Orientation Week

Breakbattle Academy

Ruby Vincent

Published by Ruby Vincent, 2019.

Chapter One

Jordan dumped the box before the threshold and flung herself on the mattress. I carefully inched through the door, hands straining to carry my bin full of books.

"You could at least make up the bed first," I said. I let the bin slip through my fingers and fall to the floor with a thump. I didn't waste time opening it and filling the empty bookshelves with the beautiful sight of multicolored spines. "The covers and sheets are in the box by the desk."

The mattress squeaked as Jordan got comfortable. "Nah, Zee, you can handle that."

I rolled my eyes as I peered over my shoulder. "If you didn't come to help with the unpacking, why are you here?"

She shot me a wounded look. "Don't be like that. I came to hang out with my favorite cousin. I haven't seen you since we were thirteen."

I wasn't moved. "We've video-chatted almost every week since I left for Southeast Asia. You're sick of my face. We both know why you really came rushing over."

Jordan put on the offended look for a few more seconds before dropping it. "Alright, fine, we do. But for the record, I'm not sick of your face. I really did miss you."

A smile tugged at my lips. "I missed you too."

Before I knew it, I had abandoned my books and crossed the room. Jordan and I enfolded each other in a hug. She was my cousin, but also my best friend and I didn't have a lot of those. A life moving from country to country with Mom meant I lost friends as quickly as I made them. My constant video calls with Jordan were what kept me sane.

"Is it weird being back home?" she asked.

I pulled away and took up a spot on the edge of the mattress. "No, not really. This was never home. Sure, we visited for Christmases, but I've spent most of my life away from Chesterfield."

"Which is why I thought you'd want to go to Chesterfield High with me. At least you'd know someone there and you could hang out with me and my friends. I don't get why you're doing this."

I cut eyes to my open door. "I'm starved," I replied, skirting the obvious question in her voice. "Let's grab something to eat and we can finish setting up my room."

I got up and walked out before she had a chance to protest. Her footsteps thundered behind me as I reached the stairs.

"But why Breakbattle?" she hissed. "That place is weird as hell. Did you check out the website? It's insane what they make the students do."

Voices floated up the stairwell. "...my office. I'm excited about this new venture into nonfiction. I will be the voice of female empowerment this generation needs."

"Glad to see you're still as modest as ever," came the amused reply.

"I'm serious, Beverly."

"I know. Trust me, I know."

Jordan and I reached the bottom steps to find our mothers looking exactly the way we expected. A frown twisted my mom's otherwise pleasant features while Aunt Beverly looked on with half fondness/half irritation.

It struck me how similar they looked. They weren't twins, but you could easily make that mistake. They both had the same pointed nose, sable eyes, and wavy brown hair—or they did before Mom shaved her head to shed the "shackles of expectations in hair length and femininity."

I glanced at Jordan. She looked like her mom too and I knew, as she got older, the resemblance would only grow stronger. She was beautiful. All three of them were beautiful women, and more than that, they looked like a family. I couldn't help but feel out of place the rare times the four of us were in the same room.

I did not look like them. Blonde crept into my genes and burnished my wavy locks into a much lighter version than theirs. My nose was snubbed rather than pointed and my eyes a light brown in place of their sable orbs. The three of them had at least three inches on me and curves for miles. I was short and thin.

I even dress differently, I thought as I took the three in. Even with their different tastes and personalities, I managed to be the odd one out. Mom in her tight, high-waisted pants and sleeveless blouse. Aunt Bev in her loose jeans and flannel, and Jordan in her tank top and skinny jeans. I was the one who favored skirts and dresses—much to Mom's chagrin. If I hadn't seen the extremely graphic and traumatizing video of my birth, I wouldn't have believed I was related to these three at all.

Aunt Beverly pulled my scowling mother in for a hug. "I'm glad you're back, Brenda—"

"It's not Brenda," Mom snapped as she escaped her hold. "I shed that name and the past she evoked. As I have told you multiple times, my name is now Andronika."

"You should also shed any delusions that I'm going to call you that."

Jordan stifled a laugh while I looked on with wide eyes. No one else dared talk to my mother like that, but Aunt Bev had the self-assurance that came with running construction sites and being the older sister. She wasn't one to be intimidated.

Beverly leveled a finger at me. "You had to pass it on to my niece too. Honestly, Brenda. Zela? You know Mom was hoping you'd name your daughter after her."

I piped up. "You can just call me Zee, Auntie. Everyone does."

Mom spun around and pinned me with her glare. "She *cannot* call you 'Zee' nor should anyone else! I went on a four-month spiritual journey to discover the name meant for my only child. Zela was the name given to me to give to you. It means you are a warrior. You lack nothing and need no one. It is a name you should be proud of."

"Yes, Mom," two voices said at once. Mine was loud and clear while Jordan mocked me under her breath.

Mom sniffed and stomped away while Aunt Bev shot me a wink before trailing after her.

I narrowed my eyes at Jordan when they were gone.

"What?" she challenged. "Every time your mom spins out, you back down and go 'yes, Mom. Sorry, Mom' until she flounces away. It's not my fault you're predictable."

Heaving a sigh, I sidestepped her and led the way to my new kitchen. We had been back in Chesterfield for a week, but our split-level bungalow was still a mess of boxes, bubble wrap, and pieces waiting to be assembled. Aunt Bev helped Mom buy the house while we were overseas, but we stepped off the plane with nothing but what fit into our single backpacks. We had to order everything new and wait as stocky deliverymen brought in the pieces that would make up our new lives.

I paused in front of the box that held our teakettle and lifted it off the counter. My eyes grew unfocused as I gazed at it. In my short fifteen-year life, I had lived in twenty-six countries. What began as a short vacation to "discover" my name, ended up with my pregnant mom traveling all over Africa meeting new people. She came back to Chesterfield to give birth to me, but during her last trimester, she completed her first fiction novel based on the people and settings she'd lived in.

That book earned her a hefty advance and saw me at seven months old on my first transatlantic flight. We had been traveling light and moving from country to country ever since.

That's a lot of different teakettles, I thought as the image of the simple metallic item stared back at me. *But no more. I'll be using the same kettle for years to come. I'll sleep in the same bed. I'll walk through the same halls and wear a tread in the carpet. Everything around me is new, but this time they'll be with me long enough to become familiar.*

"You're getting all poetic again, aren't you?" I jerked my head up to see Jordan's wry smile. "Who says math geeks are all cold and analytical?"

Cheeks warming, I tore open the box and pulled out the kettle. "I'm not a math geek and I wasn't getting poetic."

"You are a math geek," she shot back. "It's why you had to move home. Plus, you can't play me. I know you're skipping about finally being in one place. You hated all that moving around."

What I hated was how well Jordan knew me. I turned my back on her as I filled the kettle in the sink. "I didn't hate it," I said after a few seconds. "I got to visit places people only dream about and I've met the coolest people, but..."

"But your cousin is your only friend in the world because you moved around too much to make any *and* you've had to endure being homeschooled by Aunt Dronika. Trust me. I know why you're happy."

I turned the kettle on and went back to Jordan. I moved the box of towels and pot holders off the stool before taking a seat next to her. "I didn't mind being homeschooled by Mom, but it did become obvious I was years ahead in math. She didn't think she was qualified to teach me advanced mathematics and she wants to focus on her new book anyway. She agreed that high school was a good time for me to go to a traditional school."

Jordan leaned in, lowering her voice. "But you're not trying to go to a traditional school," she hissed. "You're trying to go to *Breakbattle*. Does your mom know you want to go there?"

I glanced at the kitchen entrance before whispering, "No, you're the only one I've told."

"Of course, I am, because you'd be a smear on the driveway otherwise. Your mom is going to freak! It goes against everything she believes in."

Doubt tried to creep in, but I fiercely beat it back. I had to do this. I couldn't let anyone stop me. "I know, but I have a plan. I can get her to say yes."

"How are you going to do that? No one can get Aunt Dronika to do anything she doesn't want to do." She shook her head. "Or that's what Mom says. She told me your mom used to be so happy and sweet, but she changed after your dad ditched her."

I looked away as my fists balled under the table.

"You know what I think?" Jordan's voice broke through the fog descending on my mind. "I say Mom is romanticizing the past and her little sister was always this tough. My theory is that after your mom and dad reproduced... she ate him."

A laugh ripped out of my throat unbidden. I shoved Jordan's shoulder and almost sent her toppling to the floor as I howled. "You're such an idiot," I cried.

She righted herself with a grin on her lips. "I'm serious. She is always saying how women don't need men and she's been empowered through single motherhood. I don't think your dad left. I bet she went praying mantis on the guy."

Laughing, I leaned forward and pulled her in for a hug. "I really did miss you, cuz."

She squeezed me just as tight. "I know, so... tell me why you're not going to Chesterfield High. It was all you could talk about last week when we picked you up from the airport. What changed?"

My eyes fluttered shut, but that did nothing to block the visions assaulting my mind. Something had happened. Something that had changed everything—that had changed me. No matter how Mom felt about it, I was going to Breakbattle Academy.

But no one could know why.

"I'll tell you everything," I said as I broke the hug. Well, no one could know except Jordan. It was why I spilled the beans to her in the first place. "But no one else can know."

I pushed back the memories and locked them away. "I'll tell Mom it's because I am a math geek. Chesterfield High only offers math classes up to Calculus II and I'm past that. Breakbattle has the advanced classes I'm looking for."

"Okay, but do you really think that's going to be enough? How are you going to convince her to let you go?"

"Now that... is where it gets tricky."

"GOODBYE, SWEETIE." Aunt Bev gifted me with kisses on both cheeks. "Jordan will come by tomorrow and help you unpack for real."

Jordan waggled her brows at me from the front steps. "Yep, and then after we'll go *school shopping*."

I gave her a warning look. "Sounds good. I'll see you tomorrow."

Mom waved over my shoulder. "Goodbye, Beverly. We can talk more about my book this weekend over dinner."

"Can't wait," Bev mumbled. The two stepped off the porch as Mom slammed the door shut. She heaved a sigh.

"I love her, but my sister can test the patience of a saint," Mom griped.

Why do I have a feeling Aunt Bev is saying the same thing on the other side of that door?

Mom turned and walked off. I fell in step behind her.

"Mom, can I talk to you about something?"

"Is it about dinner?" she replied without slowing down. "I'm not in the mood to cook, so you may order takeout, but nothing fried or dripping in oil. A woman must treat her mind and body as a temple. They are the sources of her power."

"Right, of course. Sources of power. I know. But that's not what I needed to talk to you about."

"What is it, Zela? I'm very busy." Mom stopped in front of glass-paned double doors and threw them open. "I want to finish the first chapter today."

I paused in the doorway while Mom went inside. Her office was the only room in the house that was done. I looked around while she took a seat at her desk. It was exactly how I pictured it would look the dozens of times she described her dream office. Her desk rested before the bay windows and sunlight cast over the paper-laden surface. Bookshelves lined the walls filled with books written by my mother and her favorite writers. Plush, brown carpet covered the floor and made the room cozy. It was a beautiful space, and one I was forbidden to step foot in.

I straightened my back as I gazed at my mother across the room. "Mom, I wanted to talk to you about my high school. I've decided where I want to go."

She didn't look at me as she opened her laptop. "I know you want to go to school with Jordan. We'll get you registered next week. Now, if that's all—"

"I don't want to go to Chesterfield High," I cut in. I took a steadying breath. "I want to go to another school. I want to go to... Breakbattle Academy."

Silence descended on the room. It wasn't broken by the sound of my breathing because I stopped doing that the moment the final word fell from my lips. Mom froze, head bent down and partially obscured.

Slowly, Mom lifted her head over the top of the laptop. Our eyes met and the look in hers made my throat dry up. "What did you just say?" she asked, voice so soft it barely carried across the room.

"If you let me explain—"

"Get in here."

I swallowed hard. "But I'm not allowed—"

"Come here. Now."

Lifting my chin, I stepped into the room and padded across the carpet. Mom rose when I stopped in front of her desk.

"What on earth would give you the idea that I would allow you to go to that place? It's everything that is wrong with our society."

"Mom—"

"It's an elitist institution built on sexism and discrimination."

"I know, Mom. I—"

She threw up her hands. "It's the very reason I'm writing this book!" she cried. "To show women that they need not be defined by the limitations others put on them. To have my own daughter tell me she wants to don a plaid skirt and skip through their segregated campus is unthinkable! I will not—"

"Mom, I want to go as a boy!"

"—allow you t-to..." Mom trailed off, blinking at me. "Excuse me? What did you say?"

I placed a hand over my clamoring heart and tried again in a lower tone. "I don't want to don a plaid skirt; I want to don a blazer. I want to enter the academy as a boy."

Mom was still gaping at me. I think this was the first time in her thirty-six years that she was struck speechless. I used that chance to get the rest out.

"You're right about that school being everything that is wrong with our society. They keep the boys and girls apart because they don't believe they can compete against each other. I want to prove them wrong."

"Why?" Mom asked when she found her voice. "Why in this way?"

I gestured at her laptop. "Because of your book. Don't you see? This is a case study. Breakbattle tells the world that they're the best—better than Evergreen Academy ever was. They sell this lie that their system is revolutionary, and that no discrimination takes place, but the boys and girls can't prove otherwise because they're kept apart. If I go in as a boy, I can see what it's really like and you can use what I learn."

The skin around her eyes crinkled as she squinted at me. I held still as though she was seeing through to my soul. "You've never shown an interest in my work before."

"Y-you've only written fiction before," I said quickly. "I couldn't help with that, but a guide for women and female empowerment I can. Breakbattle offers the most advanced classes in the county, and when I graduate top of the boy's school and reveal myself as a girl, the whole world will know the stupid rules they built the school on are crap."

Mom studied me for such a long time, my knees almost gave out when she nodded. "You're right."

I am? Oh my gosh. It's working?!

"That institution is an awful place that touts itself as the top school in the country. It should be exposed for what it really is and the damage they do." She tossed her head. "You know, your father graduated from Breakbattle."

"My dad did?" I whispered. My hands began to tremble and I quickly clasped them behind my back. "What— What class was he in?"

"The top class, of course, and it fed into his ego and ridiculous illusions that he was better than everyone and beholden to no one," she spat, venom lacing her voice. "He believed himself to be the best, but in truth, the best thing Jeremy Holt did was leave."

I said nothing. There was nothing I could say. She would not hear a word in his defense and it wasn't as though I could defend a man I didn't know. My mother's hatred of the guy who abandoned her had warped her entire being. I wish I could have known the person Aunt Beverly said she was before I came along, but I would never know that woman like I had never known my father.

Mom's face cleared as she got herself under control. She came around the desk to face me. "I think your plan is inspired, Zela," she said as she perched on the edge of the desk. "But your focus should be on your schoolwork, not on my book." She tapped my forehead. "Mind and body, Zela. That is your power."

No, I'm losing her. I have to think of something.

"I agree, Mom, but..." I quickly cast for another reason. "But I can't develop my mind at Chesterfield. They don't offer the math classes I need. Only Breakbattle does. This way, I can take advantage of their resources and use them just like they use the students."

Her expression morphed. The usual determined set to her chin shifted as she frowned. "Goodness. Chesterfield doesn't have the classes you need?"

I shook my head.

"And it's over two hours to the nearest community college," Mom continued, mostly to herself. "I can't allow you to receive a subpar education, but Breakbattle is such a loathsome school." She swore. "This must be what all the other families face. They don't want to be part of their charade, but it's either that or their children go to the underfunded local schools."

"It's how they've been getting away with it," I pressed. I didn't want to overdo it, but Mom needed to keep going in the right direction. "If I go as a boy, it could make a difference for me and the community. Maybe more people will push to mix the classes."

Mom was nodding along as my words washed over her. "Yes, yes." She stood up and patted my shoulder. "Let me think about it, Zela. I'll have an answer for you by tomorrow."

I inclined my head. "Thank you, Mom."

Mom was seated in front of her laptop by the time I backed out of the door. I waited until I was safely in my room before I let the smile break out on my face. I didn't have to wait until tomorrow. I knew my mom. I was going to Breakbattle Academy.

Chapter Two

"I still can't believe you did it!" The knob rattled. "Will you hurry up? I want to see!"

"Give me a minute, Jordan." I stood before the mirror, trying to make sense of my reflection. The changes weren't drastic, but yet I was looking at a completely different person.

Mom had been on board with the idea of me shaving my head, but I opted for a wig instead. It matched my hair color but hung down low over my forehead to conceal my plucked eyebrows. It was the clothes though that afforded the biggest change. It was amazing how switching out a dress and a pair of heels for a long-sleeved tee and a plain shirt had effectively switched me out for someone else.

Bang! Bang! Bang!

"Zela Manning, get out here now!"

Groaning, I whirled away from the mirror and yanked open the door on my irritating cousin. Her mouth fell open.

"Oh my gosh," she breathed. "I'm a genius."

"Taking all the credit, I see."

"I deserve the credit. I'm the one who picked out your clothes and your wig. Unsurprisingly, you don't have a clue how the average American guy dresses."

"I pick up one beanie and you think I'm hopeless."

I brushed past her and made for my bed. The past month since I moved in had seen this bare space transformed into the bedroom I always wanted. Photos and trinkets from my travels decorated the walls and almost every available surface. My bed was decked out in pink silk sheets that perfectly matched the pink rug and desk chair.

I had put so much effort into getting my first real bedroom the way I wanted it and now I would have to leave.

"I can't believe I'm off to boarding school today." I bent and picked up a black duffel bag at the foot of my bed. My *new* clothes covered my bedspread. There was even a mound of boxers as a result of Jordan getting carried away.

Jordan flopped down on my pile of white tees. "At least you only have to stay there Monday through Friday. You'll come home every weekend and tell me about the hot guys you're bringing back to your dorm."

I rolled my eyes. "How many times do I have to tell you this isn't about picking up guys?"

She flapped a hand. "Yeah, yeah. I know about your mission, but may I remind you, you're a willing young virgin about to step into a den of boys." Jordan's eyes glittered as her fantasies worked overtime. "You'll be sleeping in their dorm. You'll be eating with them. You'll be in their locker room."

I stiffened, cheeks heating up. A month of planning for this and the words "locker room" hadn't crossed my mind until that moment.

Jordan must have picked up my panic because she got even more gleeful. "You poor little homeschooler. You didn't think about that, did you? You'll be seeing all that manflesh."

"There won't be any manflesh!" I squeaked. "I've seen the website. They have private showers."

Her smile didn't go anywhere. "In the dorms, cuz. Not in the gym. One of my friends has an older sister that got into Breakbattle. I pumped her for info and, let me just say, I'm jealous."

I ducked my head, letting my new hair fall over my eyes as I shoved my clothes into the duffel bag. This was not good. I hadn't even set foot on the campus and I had already run into a problem.

"What am I going to do?" I whispered.

"What did I just say?" She shoved my shoulder. "Willing young virgin, you're going to partake."

"I'm not going to— Who said— I'm not willing!" I finally got out. "No one is partaking in anything. They can't know I'm a girl or they'll kick me over to the girls' side of the campus. I'll just have to think of an excuse to stay out of the locker room."

She waved that away. "Sweetie, I'm sure your boyfriends will keep your secret. They wouldn't want you to be kicked off campus either. When you stay at my place over the weekends, you'll tell me all about them."

Despite myself, I laughed. "Them? Now I've gone from a virgin to running multiple secret boyfriends? You need to slow down on the fantasies, Jordan. I told you this isn't about guys."

She plugged her ears. "I'm not listening to you," she half-shouted. "You're not ruining this for me. If Mom hadn't shut me down, I'd be buttoning up my blazer and joining you."

As if summoned, Aunt Bev's voice sounded on the other side of my door. "...nonsense. I can't believe you're letting her do this!"

"She's my daughter, Beverly," I heard Mom say. "I happen to think this will be a great learning experience for her in more ways than one."

"That's a load of crock!" My door banged open, making me jump. Beverly stormed into the bedroom with my mom on her heels. She took one look at me in my new getup and her eyes bugged out. "Zee, for the love of all that's good! Why are you doing this?"

"This is the only way I can take the classes I need, Auntie." The lie fell from my lips so easily now. "Plus, I can show Break-battle up. It's not cool how they separate the boys and girls."

Of course, it wasn't, but my need to be at this school was much bigger than that. I had to go even if it meant incurring Aunt Bev's disapproval.

"No, it's not," she agreed, "but they have their reasons and you don't need to go this far to prove they're wrong."

My mom stepped forward. "Beverly, that's enough." She held out her hand. "Give me the keys and I'll take her there myself."

"Not a chance, Brenda. I've still got a half hour car ride to talk her out of this foolishness and I'm taking full advantage of it. If you don't like it, you should have gotten your own car." She turned and marched out.

Huffing, Mom went after her. "I *will* get my own car. I..."

Jordan shook her head at the empty doorway. "It's hard to believe those two are related. You and I are much better at this sister thing."

I held back a smile. Jordan did feel like my sister at times. Of all the friends I had made on the road, she was the only one to answer every video chat and sit and talk with me for hours.

Those friends had faded from my life, but Jordan stuck around. Some might think it was because she was family, but I've come across all sorts of families from all over the world and plenty of them were more than happy to ignore their relatives. Jordan really cared. She cared so much she still supported me even though she knew what really happened the day after I moved into my new home... and what I planned to do about it.

My jeans crumpled in my fists as a surge of pain and anger choked me. *Focus, Zela. Channel this into something useful.*

"Help me with this," I croaked. "Orientation starts at eight on the dot. I can't be late."

"DO YOU PROMISE YOU'LL come home every weekend?" Jordan asked. She reached across the seat and took my hand. "I'm not going back to only seeing you at holidays."

"Of course, I'll come home. Why would I want to spend my weekends at school? The place would probably be deserted since all the other kids will run off to have a life."

She squeezed my hand, looking satisfied.

"I don't see what the point of that is," Aunt Bev spoke up from the driver's seat. "Why have a boarding school that only keeps the students on the weekdays?"

Jordan shrugged. "How else is their freaky system supposed to work? They'd need to keep the students after school, or otherwise, they would always be interrupting classes."

Mom twisted around in her seat. "That is an excellent point. Another indictment of the harm their system causes. Young women are forced to spend less time with their families and outside peers so they can be subjected to their draconian rules." She nodded. "Draconian. That's going into the book." Mom turned her gaze on me. "Make sure you call me with regular updates, Zela. Don't wait until the weekends. Also, see if you can interview some of the girls and—"

"Honestly, Brenda," Auntie snapped. "She is *not* your spy. If you want to interview the students, go through the proper channels like a normal person."

"My name is not Brenda!"

The two fell into a shouting match as Jordan and I threw each other a look in the back seat. There was no point getting in the middle of it. They would keep going until they ran out of steam.

Mom and Aunt Beverly didn't take a break from their argument until we turned on to Battle Street. Traffic slowed to a dead stop. The one-way road was lined with cars all heading for one place.

I leaned forward until Mom's seat stopped me. The sight of Breakbattle gripped me and drew me in.

"Wow," I breathed.

The school was even more incredible than the brochures suggested. The structure took over the horizon, demanding to be seen like the majestic cathedrals I walked among in Europe, but Breakbattle rivaled their size. The school itself took up most of the ten acres they boasted about, but if the website was to be believed, there was also a swimming pool, courts, and a track behind it.

"Wow," Jordan echoed from my other side. "Mom, are you sure I can't go here too?"

"What are you talking about? You are excited about going to high school with your friends. Besides, it's too late to get you signed up for orientation."

Orientation.

The word rattled around in my brain as we got closer and closer to Breakbattle. I was about to step into an auditorium full of guys with my chest wrapped up and a wig on my head. What if they saw right through me? How was I supposed to fool them? What did I know about guys? I didn't have brothers, male cousins, or an uncle anymore since Jordan's dad passed away when we were nine.

There's no way I'm going to pull this off. They'll find me out. Kick me to the other side and then the whole school will brand me as the weirdo who pretended to be a boy so she could sneak into the lockers and see manflesh. This was going to blow up in my face.

I slipped into a downward spiral as Auntie made it to the parking lot and pulled into a spot. Jordan had to come around to my door and pull me out.

"What's up? Are you freaking?"

"Yes, yes, and *yes*," I hissed. "What the hell am I doing here?"

She laughed. "Relax. No one is going to pick you out as a girl. In this case, your complete lack of boobs and womanly curves is working for you."

"Just for that, I'm not telling you about my boyfriends."

"No, no. I take it back." Laughing, she threw her arm around my shoulder and led me to the trunk. "Just lower your voice like we practiced. Angle away when guys come in for that chest bump thing they like to do, and lock up your feminine products."

I bobbed my head, beating back anxiety as I reached for my bag.

"You're going to be fine. Don't worry."

Aunt Bev came around to join us. "It's not too late to take off those clothes and turn around."

I straightened, injecting steel into my spine. "Yes, it is, Auntie. I'm doing this. Let's go."

No more was said as the four of us followed the crowd of people heading onto the grounds. On the first day of orientation, family members were given their own tour to learn more about the school and how it operated, but at one o'clock that afternoon, my family would leave and I would spend the rest of the week alone... in a den full of boys.

Together, we set foot on the sprawling campus. Breakbattle was just as gorgeous up close. Whoever they had managing the grounds took great pride in their work. Flower gardens dotted the lawn, broken up by winding cobblestone paths all leading to one place.

We walked up one of the paths to the tables set up on the lawn. A volunteer shot me a beaming smile when my shadow fell over her.

"Good morning. What's your name?"

"It's—" I stopped and cleared my throat, lowering it the way we practiced. "It's Manning. Zeke Manning."

"Welcome to Breakbattle Academy, Zeke Manning."

I STUMBLED THROUGH the halls, struggling to control my rapid breathing. Sweat was collecting beneath my bindings and I already longed to rip them off. I was separated from

Mom, Aunt Bev, and Jordan almost immediately. After checking in, the volunteer told them to go one way and me another. Their tour would start with refreshments in the cafeteria and then a lovely stroll through the grounds, while I was supposed to report to the auditorium five minutes ago.

My heart pounded as I looked at my watch. *This place is a freaking maze. How am I supposed to find anything?*

Panicked as I was, I could only give the checkered floors, paneled walls, and looming portraits a passing glance. I didn't have time to take in the stately charm of the school.

Where is—

"Over here, man. It's this way."

My ears perked up at the voice. I hitched my bag higher up my shoulder and picked up the pace. Rounding the corner, I spotted two guys as they disappeared through a set of double doors. This had to be the place.

I walked up and the sign over the entrance confirmed it. Looking into the auditorium I could see most of the room was already seated.

Another table of volunteers were set up by the doors and I moved over to them. The two guys behind the table were a lot younger and looked way more bored. One of them was on their phone and he didn't bother to glance up when I said hello.

The other rose as his lips stretched into a smile. My breath caught as I got a proper look at him. If you had told me he had just walked off the stage at Fashion Week, I would have had no trouble believing it even with the school uniform. Angels must have sculpted his strong jaw, cleft chin, aquiline nose, and large brown eyes for the sole purpose of stealing the breath from innocents.

His lips moved. It wasn't until his forehead wrinkled that I remembered what that meant.

I shook myself. "What? What did you say?"

"I said you can leave your bag there." He pointed over my shoulder. "You'll take it to your rooms after the opening ceremony. What's your name?"

"Zel— Zeke Manning."

He nodded as he bent over the nametags. The guy plucked one off the table and handed it to me. "You're in group 3G. Everything is alphabetical. Your roommate, seat assignment, and everything else." The guy rattled off instructions without pausing for air. "Each group is led by two group leaders and we're yours. If you need help, come to us. Any questions?"

"Um..." I glanced around the cavernous space and the back of the heads of the guys who would be my new classmates. My eyes soon drifted back to Gorgeous. This guy seemed nice enough and he wasn't giving me crazy looks or shouting for administration so I was clearly passing for a boy in front of him.

"What's your name?" I finally asked.

The guy chuckled. It was a low, husky sound that made goose pimples erupt on my skin.

"You'll find out soon enough, dude." He gestured with his chin. "Take your seat."

I frowned at the odd response but quickly got into gear when I heard someone tap the microphone. I dropped my bag among the suitcases and made a beeline for the chairs, scanning the signs on the way.

"Good morning, students. On behalf of the entire administration, we welcome you to Breakbattle Academy."

Applause broke out as I scurried down the aisle. It was a relief when I spotted the sign that read 3G. My group had ended up in the middle rows. There was a single empty seat on the aisle and I plopped down. Only then did I look up at the stage.

A smartly dressed woman stood before the podium. Middle-aged, but quite pretty and stylish from her chic pixie-cut and form-fitting pantsuit. Behind her, members of staff sat in high-backed chairs looking on at the new class.

"...introduce myself," the speaker continued. "I am your vice principal, Mrs. Argyle. Tonight, at the opening dinner, your principal and members of staff hope to get to know you in a more casual setting, but for now, we will introduce ourselves and then we'll get into what will be expected of you beginning September first."

Argyle stepped back and, one by one, the people in the chairs walked up to the podium and stated their names and gave quick intros. It wasn't more than two sentences to say their positions and that they were looking forward to the coming year. That was until the guy in the last seat stood and strolled across the stage.

He was tall. He had at least a foot on Argyle and she was no shorty. He was also handsome with a full head of salt-and-pepper hair and glasses that were trendier than the ones you caught on men his age.

He didn't speak at first, and the silence spread as his blinding smile was leveled at everyone in the room. "Hello, gentlemen," he finally began. "I am Principal Whittaker and looking at all of you, I have no doubt we are heading into an astounding year. I see the intelligence in your eyes and the talent in your blood. Use it!"

I jerked when his fist smacked the podium, ringing through the speakers. A snort to my right told me I was being laughed at.

"Use it to bring this school and yourselves to even greater heights. You have a unique opportunity that no other student in the country— No. That no one in the world has. Breakbattle was born under the revolutionary idea that there is no such thing as 'standard' education." Whittaker's eyes were shining like headlamps and it wasn't because of the harsh lighting.

"Why would there be when there is no such thing as standard people. We are all different. We have different skills, different capabilities, and when we enter adulthood, we will have to use those abilities to fight for everything we have or hope to get. An education that does not prepare you for that battle is a failed one.

"At Breakbattle, you will receive that preparation and some of you will go on to join the prominent alumni that are honored in our halls... and some of you won't."

I blinked. *Wait? What did he just say?*

"How far you will go in Breakbattle is dependent on the same factor that determines how far you will go in life: you. So never rest, never give up, and never stop fighting, because this is a climb you must make on your own."

He paused, smile dimming as he grew serious. His eyes swept through the room and I could have sworn they landed on me—searching, assessing, and measuring before moving on.

"Thank you, gentlemen," he finished. "I know you won't let me down."

"Well said, Principal Whittaker." Argyle clapped enthusiastically as she retook her place. The boys joined in, but my hands remained in my lap. The fervor in his eyes told me louder than words how serious this place was. What did I get myself into?

"Alright, everyone," Argyle continued. "Let's speak more about what will happen this week."

I chanced a look down the row while she was talking. All of the guys were paying rapt attention to the stage, but my fidgeting made the guy next to me break away and meet my eyes. Mine widened as brown met green. I swallowed hard as he gave me a slight smile and a nod before looking away.

Goodness, is everyone here gorgeous?

"As I hope you know, this week is not about determining acceptance," Mrs. Argyle said as I tuned back in. "You have all been accepted into Breakbattle and you will attend in the fall. No, this week is solely about determining your placement and which class is the best fit for your talents and abilities."

I leaned back in my seat. She suddenly had my full attention as well.

"Here in Breakbattle, we don't believe in a one-size-fits-all approach. This will not be your reality when you move on to college and your careers, and if it is our job to prepare you for that, we must do so by structuring your lessons to your needs.

"Each grade is split into six classes. There is the F Class, D Class, C Class, B Class, A Class, and finally, the Elite Class. Which class you will end up in will be decided based on how you perform over the coming week and on the placement test that will be taken on your last day.

"It should come as no surprise that each class is different from the other—as are the privileges that go with them. Hard work reaps benefits, and at Breakbattle, we reward that dedication by giving you those benefits.

"As for the battle system," she continued, "I will not go into detail about that at this time. Battles are not to be held during orientation week. When school starts in the fall, you will be taught everything you need to know about the system and its rules, but this week, we need you focused on getting into the classes that are appropriate for you."

I let Argyle's speech wash over me as I sank into my seat. I had heard bits and pieces of the battle system from Mom and Jordan, but I was hoping to find out the full extent of what I was in for.

Maybe there is a reason they won't tell us during orientation. It gives us too much time to beat it out of here for another school before we're officially enrolled.

But I'm not going anywhere, a voice reminded me. *This is where I need to be.*

The vice principal went over the schedule for the week and gave us the rundown of the rules. I was listening with half an ear until Argyle stepped around the podium.

"You have been split into five groups and each group has two team leaders. You are in for a treat because for this orientation, the rising sophomore Elite Class have volunteered to be your leaders." Even from halfway down the auditorium, I spotted Argyle's chest puff with pride. "Boys, if you will please stand and come onto the stage."

All over the room, random guys got to their feet and made their way up the stage. I blinked when I realized two of them were familiar.

Gorgeous and Bored Guy led the pack as the ten of them lined up before the room.

"The Elite Class is capped at no more than ten students," said Argyle. "These are the boys that placed in the top percentile and continue to show their excellence in all that they do." The pride wasn't just puffing her chest. It laced her every word. "To be in the Elite Class is not an honor given to you, it is one you must strive for and earn on your own merit. Think of that as you go through this week and let it drive you. Now, let me introduce your leaders so we can officially begin the day."

I passed over their faces as she announced the boys. Varying heights, shapes, ethnicities, and looks, but all of them had one thing in common. Each of their perfectly pressed uniforms had a large patch on the breast. It was the crest of the school and in the middle was a large E.

Argyle placed her hand on Bored Guy's shoulder. Now that his face wasn't stuck to his phone, I could see he kept with the tradition of the school and was more handsome than a guy should be. Jet-black locks framed his face, curling at the ends in the cutest way. He was no small guy. Broad shoulders made his blazer stretch to the seams and Argyle had to lift her hand over her head to reach them.

"This is Santiago Holland," she said. "Santiago achieved the highest math score in Breakbattle history on the placement test, and in the year since he has been here, he has led the math team to two victories in the Archimedean state and regional competitions."

Despite the praise she was heaping on him, Santiago's striking amber eyes held nothing but disinterest. She patted his arm before moving to the final boy in the row.

"Cameron Dupre holds the highest grade point average in the rising sophomore class and is captain of our champion basketball team. The youngest captain in Breakbattle history."

Cameron inclined his head, smiling that perfect smile.

Argyle stepped to his side and gestured down the row of boys. "They have graciously given up part of their summer to volunteer, so take advantage by learning all that you can from them. Principal Whittaker was right; this will be a great year."

The auditorium broke into applause once more, signaling the end of the opening ceremony. It was the first day, so according to the schedule, all we had to do was unpack in our rooms, go on a campus tour, and then the real fun happened at the opening feast when we were allowed to mingle and get to know each other.

I rose from my seat along with everyone else and shuffled toward the luggage. Someone tapped me on the back as I bent for my duffel. Peering through my hair, I laid eyes on the guy I was sitting next to.

"Hey," he said. His lips curled into a grin that brought a dimple to his cheeks. "I think we're in the same group."

"Yeah. Nice to meet you." I straightened and stuck out my hand. "I'm Zeke Manning."

"Manning?" he asked as he shook. "We might be roommates. What's your badge say?"

"My badge?"

He pointed. "On the back."

Glancing down, I flipped over my nametag and saw "Floor Five, Rm 561." I showed it to him.

His grin got even wider. "Sweet, we are roommates. I'm Adam Moon. It looks like it's me and you this week."

I relaxed under his friendliness. "Sounds good to me, Adam."

"Group 3G! Hustle up!"

Adam dropped my hand at the shout and hurried to get his stuff. It took me only a second to find Cameron and Santiago over the heads of the crowd, waiting for my group.

Adam and I pushed through and planted ourselves in front of the guys. When everyone was there, Cameron spoke.

"So you heard Argyle," he announced. "You'll have an hour to unpack and then you'll meet me and Santi outside the dorms for a tour of campus. Afterward, we'll bring you to the cafeteria where your family will be waiting. Eat, say your goodbyes, and then"—Cameron cut eyes to Santiago who suddenly had the same grin on his face as him—"get ready for the week of your life."

My brows snapped together. Was it me, or was there something behind those smiles?

I glanced around at the other boys, but everyone else appeared relaxed or excited.

You're imagining things, Zela. You're just on edge because if any one of these guys finds you out, it's all over. Remember why you're here.

The internal pep talk steadied me. Everything was fine. All that mattered is what I came here for.

"Let's go."

Cameron and Santiago led the way out of the room and we followed behind like little ducklings.

"The building is shaped like an unused staple," Cameron called over his shoulder. "The boys get the left wing. The girls in the right wing. The administration office and cafeteria in the middle. You shouldn't get lost, but there are maps in your welcome packets if you need them. Any questions?"

Someone knocked my shoulder as they moved up front. The guy sported thick glasses and wore eagerness as plain as his woolen coat. "Cameron, are you really the top of the Elite Class? How did you do it?"

Cameron didn't slow his stride. "By being better than everyone else."

My eyebrows shot up to my fake hairline. Was this guy for real?

A boy piped up from behind me. "I heard the math placement test gets harder as you go. All the way to graduate-level mathematics. And, Santiago, you got the highest math score in Breakbattle history?"

Santiago grunted by way of response.

"Does this guy speak?" The question slipped out under my breath before I could think about it.

"He does, but not to say anything interesting."

My head whipped around in surprise, catching Adam's grin.

"Cameron," someone said. "What's it like being in the Elite Class?"

Adam grabbed my arm. "Come on. Let's hang back while the others fall all over them."

We stopped and let the group move on ahead, bringing up the back.

I smiled at Adam. "I take it you know them."

"Cam and Santi, yeah. We went to Evergreen Middle School together, but they were a year ahead. I know most of the guys here. A lot of them are from my town."

"That must be nice. I don't know anyone here," I replied as I looked around. Now that I wasn't rushing about like a headless chicken, I could take in the space. Large windows had been cracked open to let in the fresh summer air and they looked down on to a grassy area and the tour group assembled outside. I knew Mom, Jordan, and Aunt Bev were in there somewhere.

"It's cool, I guess," said Adam. "This is the only decent boarding school that people in my town will send their kids to, so most of my friends are here."

I turned my head and gave Adam a proper look. His head was a mop of soft brown curls that he flicked out of his eye every five seconds. They just fell right back, which was a shame because his eyes were a striking emerald green. It was hard to choose between staring at those eyes or at his charming smile. A smile that hadn't left his face since I met him.

"Your friends must have filled you in, then," I said, "on what it's like here."

"They did. So did my parents. Anything you want to know, I'm happy to share."

"I'm so very glad I met you, Adam Moon."

He laughed. "Alright, man. It's cool to meet you too."

I winced internally. His reaction said I was getting a little too excited at making a new friend. I needed to tone it down—be more *boy*.

Be more boy. Be more boy.

I peeked at Adam again, studying his loping stride. I straightened my back and tried to mimic his walk.

Be more boy. Be chill. Chin up. Hunch my shoulders a bit. Wider steps.

After a few tries, I had it down. *Perfect. I look just like—*

"Dude, you okay?"

I jerked. "What?"

Adam looked me up and down. "You're walking like you need to take a shit." He pointed over his shoulder. "We just passed the bathrooms. I'll wait while you go."

Face flaming, I quickly fixed myself. "I'm fine," I mumbled. "So you said you'd tell me about the school."

"For sure. What do you want to know?"

I turned toward the windows again. Cameron said the wing I was gazing at was for the girls.

"What do you think about the girls being on the other side?"

"Mom and Dads hated it," he replied. "The only times the guys and girls mix are during breakfast and dinner. Otherwise, they might as well be in a different school. I don't like it either."

I turned in time to see a strange expression cross his face. It was gone the moment he caught me looking, and the genial smile returned.

"Okay, guys, the dorms are through here."

I looked up at Cameron's voice. The group had gotten ahead of us and gathered in front of double doors that led to a separate part of the building.

"The code to get in is 1349," he said. "Your room assignments are on the nametags. Like I said, you have one hour to unpack and chill and then meet us right here so we can show you around."

Santiago typed in the code and then both boys held open the doors for us to stream in. I followed behind, but as I passed Santiago, a thought occurred to me. I paused in front of him.

"Will we get to learn more about the clubs and teams this week?"

His eyes flicked down at me. He looked for a second like he couldn't understand why I was talking to him. After a minute, he nodded.

"Great because I really want to join the math club Vice Principal Argyle was talking about. Can you tell me more about it later?"

A laugh behind me drew my attention. Cameron threw me that knee-wobbling smile when I turned to face him. "That club is for Class Bs and up. It's best to get through O-Week first to see if it's even worth the conversation."

I frowned but shrugged all the same. "Fine. Later, then." I kept going and found Adam waiting for me before the staircase. The rest of the guys had either continued on to the rooms on the first floor or were tromping up to the ones above. Together we made the trek up to the fifth.

"We're lucky," Adam said when we topped the third-floor landing.

"We are?" I huffed. My shoulder was already aching from carrying the duffel bag. "How?"

"The fifth floor has the A Class dorms. Those are the second-best rooms in the school."

I perked up. That did sound nice.

We made it up the rest of the way and then pushed through a single door into a wide hallway. The décor was much the same as the rest of the school. White paneled walls and checkered floors. We weaved through the other boys and found our room.

I made it two steps inside before shock pinned me to the carpet. If this was second best, then seeing the best might have knocked me out cold.

The room was huge. Big enough to accommodate two desks, two bookshelves, a sitting area with two loveseats, a flat-screen, two wardrobes, and two queen-size four-poster beds.

A light flicked on and I turned as Adam walked into the bathroom. I spotted the frosted glass of the shower before he closed the door.

We have a bathroom? This is perfect. If I get into A Class, I won't have to worry about the locker room or my roommate finding me out. I'll just run back here to change and do what I need to do.

I walked further inside, still taking everything in. *I wonder what the other dorms are like.*

I put my bag down and sat on the loveseat, getting comfortable. I could get used to this.

"Hey," Adam called when he came out of the bathroom. "Do you mind if I take the bed by the window?"

"It's all yours." I pulled my feet onto the loveseat and curled them under me. "So what do I have to do to make sure I'm in this dorm in the fall?"

His chuckle reached my ears. "The same thing we're all trying to do. Kick ass in the trials and then nail the placement test." I heard his footsteps as he came to join me. Adam sat in the other loveseat, legs splayed out in front of him. One look at him and I put my feet back down on the carpet.

Be more boy, Zeke!

"Most of the guys from my middle school got their class picked out too," he went on. "Everyone is hoping for B or higher, but some of them aren't settling for less than the Elite Class."

"What do they have to do to get in? What do we all have to do? What are the trials?"

Laughing, he threw up his hands. "Hold up, dude. Give me a chance."

"Sorry. I looked over every inch of the website, but it didn't say much about what we do this week or about the battle system."

He inclined his head. "For good reason. It's kind of intense and they don't want to scare people away. Over the next couple days, we'll be running, jumping, swimming, throwing, and competing in the sports used for the physical tests. Those are the trials."

My jaw dropped. "We'll be what?!"

"Yep. Starting tomorrow and straight through to Friday. We have Saturday off to rest and then Sunday we take the placement test."

"But why? Why are we taking physical tests?"

"It's all a part of how they decide what class we'll be in," he replied. "That's what Breakbattle is all about—students who are smart, but also in peak physical condition. It's what the battles are based on."

I leaned forward, hanging on his every word. "What is a battle?"

"It's like they said this morning. In the real world, we fight for everything and we'll be doing the same here."

My eyes widened. "What do you mean fight? I thought battle was just a cute term? They don't really make us fight each other, do they?"

"Not like how you're thinking. It's just— Pretty much we—" He stopped, face scrunching up as he thought. "Okay. It's like this." He scooted forward until we were inches apart. "Let's say you get into that math club you were talking about before."

I nodded. "Okay."

"Well, the clubs here have limited space. The math club only allows fifteen students. It's full up and I want to get in. The only way for me to do that is to challenge one of the members to a battle."

"I'm with you," I said. "So you challenge me to a battle to get into the club."

"Yes. I challenge you to a test in my best subject: English. Since you were the one who was challenged, you get to pick the physical test. We have to do both. Academic test and physical test."

"Okay," I said slowly. "So I have to do my best subject for the academic test? So I'd challenge everyone to a math test?"

"You don't have to choose math, but you want to win, so everyone goes with their best subject."

"Makes sense. What about the physical tests? What are they?"

"There are only five options for that. You can race, play soccer, play basketball, wrestle, or swim."

I made a face. "Why only those five?"

He shrugged. "That's just how it works."

"Alright. So, if someone comes up to me and challenges me to a race, what—"

I stopped at his headshake. "No, the challenger picks the academic test and the challengee picks the physical test. Those are the rules."

My head was spinning trying to keep up with everything he was telling me, but I had to keep it straight. "What do I do if I get challenged to a battle?"

"You report it to a teacher and the coach. They have to supervise both tests to make sure there's no cheating and that the loser holds up their end. If it's not supervised, it doesn't count."

"Okay." I leaned back in the chair, letting my head fall onto the cushion. "What an interesting way to run a school, but it sounds like a hassle. I'm guessing battles must not happen very often."

Adam's snort brought my head back up. The look he was giving me made my stomach twist. "Are you kidding? There are battles almost every day of the school year. Sometimes up to five in one day."

I gaped at him. "Five? But why? Who would want to take more tests than they have to? Who would want to spend their free time running and jumping all over the place?"

His expression morphed into one that was bordering on pitying. "You really don't know what you've got yourself into, do you? They make us compete for pretty much everything, Zeke. Spots on field trips, volunteer opportunities, tutors, library time, computer time, office hours, getting into clubs, getting on teams."

My eyes widened as the list grew. He couldn't be serious. "Adam, the joke is over. There is no way they'd make us fight over all that stuff. Library times? Office hours? They can't limit that."

"They can, and they do." The genial smile was nowhere to be seen. I shut my mouth at the seriousness on his face. "The Elite Class and the A Class get first dibs, but after that, if we want it, we battle for it."

"But what are the rules?" I cried. "We can't battle over *everything*, right? I mean, someone couldn't challenge me for all the money in my pur— wallet," I quickly amended.

Dammit, Zela. Be careful.

Thankfully, Adam didn't seem to notice. "Actually, they can't. That is one of the rules. Battles cannot involve money, breaking school rules, or anything illegal. You also can't be challenged to do something that would hurt you. Like telling you to purposely flunk a test or be late to class and get detention. The teachers have to know what you're battling over so no one can get you to do something awful. The battle would be rejected."

"Well, that's something at least, but still. What if I don't want to do the battle at all?"

He was shaking his head before I finished the question. "If you turn down a battle, it's an automatic ten points off your final grade, every time. You refuse enough of them and you'll end up flunking out."

"Is there at least a limit to how many battles I can be challenged to?"

"Nope. You could be challenged a hundred times a semester, but that's not likely," he rushed to add, no doubt seeing the look on my face. "You'd have to have something someone wanted *and* they'd have to believe they'd win the battle. They won't waste their time if they can't win."

That made me feel marginally better, but the tight ball in my stomach hadn't quite loosened. I was a smart girl—Mom made sure of that. She'd done a great job homeschooling me and I trusted that I could hold my own in academics and crush everyone in math, but the physical tests...

Mom's ideal of strengthening the body was a healthy diet, daily yoga, Pilates, and the three months of Tae Kwon Do I learned while we lived in South Korea. I had played soccer and basketball, but only a friendly game when I ran into kids my age. I could swim, but I sucked at treading water. My lungs burned into cinders if I ran for longer than twenty feet and I had never wrestled in my life.

If someone challenged me, how could I hope to win?

The thought pulled a question from my lips. "How do you win a battle? What if I win the academic test, but fail the physical one?"

He pulled a face. "That's tough to answer because it depends. Academic tests are weighted more so you might still win the battle, but in the end, the judges will decide. They have a whole system for determining the winner in every case."

"I feel like I should be writing this down." I sighed. "You said before that the Elite Class gets first dibs. What else do they get?"

He threw out his hands. "They get rooms even nicer than this, but they don't have to share. There's only ten of them in each class so they get the whole top floor to themselves. They're like the top five percentile so not only do they get privileges from the school, but universities fall over themselves to offer them scholarships or scout them for their teams."

I bobbed my head. "They're the ones who have everything the other students want. They must be in battles every day."

"Actually, they get another advantage there too. They call it 'choosing your champion.' If you challenge someone in the Elite Class to a battle, they can face you themselves or ask someone else in their class to do it for them."

"Are you serious? But no one else can do that, can they? You said everyone else loses points if they don't do a battle."

"Yep. It's not fair, but the system isn't based on fairness. If you want to take on an Elite, you have to be ready to take them all on. Cameron dominates in biology and basketball, but if you challenge him thinking you'll crush him in math, then he'll just ask Santi to take over. Same thing for every subject. They get their best to battle for them so students outside of the A Class don't think about challenging them. They get to have everything *and* they get to keep it."

I nodded slowly, thinking about what this meant for me. "So the easiest way to get through Breakbattle is to get into the Elite Class. I'd have my own room. I wouldn't have to worry about the physical tests. I'd... even be in the same class my dad was," I whispered.

"What was that?"

"Nothing." I shook myself, coming back to reality. "I was just saying that I have to get into the Elite Class."

"That is what everyone on this campus is saying. The competition is brutal and it never stops. The next four years are going to be intense."

I blew out a breath. "I definitely didn't know what I was getting into, but you know so much."

"You will too. In the fall, they'll give us a guide that explains the system and how it works better than me."

Adam explained it pretty well, but there was still one more question nagging away at me.

"Alright, but why do they separate—"

Ring. Ring.

"One sec, man." Adam heaved himself out of the chair and rescued his phone from his backpack. "Hey, Dad. It's going great. We're staying in the A dorms. Yeah, they're sweet. My friend Zeke and I are shooting for A Class now."

It wasn't cool to listen in on other people's phone calls, but I'd be lying if I said a tiny thrill didn't go through me at being called his friend.

"No," said Adam. He stuck the phone in the crook of his ear and began unpacking. It suddenly occurred to me that I should be doing the same. We had to go down and meet Cameron and Santiago soon. "Yes. Mom's fine, Jaxson. How is she going to overdo it? She sits around all day. You know I'll be there for her."

I let Adam's chatter fade into the background as I opened my duffel bag. The large ornate wardrobe easily fit the few clothes I brought, and since I wasn't lugging makeup and perfumes, I set out my toiletries in less than a minute. I didn't come to a stuttering halt until I gazed down at the box of pads lying innocently at the bottom of my bag.

I peeked at Adam through my lashes. The guy was completely oblivious and focused on his phone call.

It's not like he'll go through my things, right? He's a nice guy.

I zipped the bag closed and stuffed it under my bed. It'll be fine. If they hadn't found me out already, then my disguise was working. As long as I didn't slip up, I'd be able to do what I came here to do.

By the time Adam finished his call, it was time to go back down. Cameron and Santiago were waiting in the spot they promised. They didn't seem too excited about their job as volunteers, but they did it well.

The two led our group of twenty on a tour of the school, showing us where the classrooms, lunchroom, and administration were. The inside tour ended in front of the principal's office. Any further and we would go over to the girls' side which was not a part of the tour. Instead, we went through the back doors and spilled out onto a verdant, sprawling quad.

Breakbattle sat on ten acres, and as my eyes swept over them trying to take in everything at once, I could see they had used them well. Patches of flower gardens lined the building. There were more cobblestone paths and they led to different structures.

"Okay, guys," said Cameron. He pointed to the buildings. "That's the gym. That's the swimming pool. The basketball courts are in there and behind all of that is the track and soccer field. You can go and check them out if you want. Just meet us back here in twenty minutes."

The group broke apart. I stuck with Adam, but I wasn't the only one who wanted to hang with him. Three guys peeled themselves out of the pack and descended on him.

"Adam!" A tall, gangly kid with a wicked smile seized him and they bumped chests. Adam did the same with the other two.

I absentmindedly rubbed my hand over my bindings. *It would hurt to be doing that all day. Jordan was right about that.*

"So they actually let you in here, Moon?" Tall Guy asked. "They're letting the standards slip."

Adam socked his shoulder. "They let everyone in, but they for sure should have made an exception with you."

"Hey, what dorm are you in? I'm in the D Class dorms and they're shit. If that's not motivation to place higher, then I don't know what is."

"I'm saying," Adam replied. "I was just telling my dad I'm getting into the A Class. Those rooms are sweet."

The four of them yukked it up while I stood there awkwardly. *I should go and let him hang with his friends. I'll go check out the gym or something.*

I made it two steps before—

"Zeke, where are you going? Come and meet my friends." A hand grasped my arm and tugged me back. Adam threw his arm around my shoulder and his heady scent engulfed me. He pointed at Tall Guy. "This is Zachary Fields." Then he moved on to a shorter, stocky boy with a dusting of freckles on his cheek. "This is Justin Samuels." The last guy sported long, brown hair held back with a single tie and an arm in a blue sling. "This is Owen Price."

I gave a little wave. "Nice to meet you."

"Sup, Zeke." Zachary grabbed my outstretched hand and pulled me in. Before I had time to think, he smashed his chest against mine. I twisted away when the others came in to do the same.

"What happened to your arm?" Adam asked.

Owen groaned. "I wrecked it falling off my skateboard. I'll be in D Class for sure because of this. I won't be able to do most of the trials."

"What?" I piped up. "They can't do that. It's not your fault."

"My mom tried that argument, but they said no exceptions. It's all about how you score. If I can't do a trial, I get a zero."

No one said anything in reply. What was there to say? One talk with Adam and I got the lesson. The competition is everything here and not being able to compete meant life would be a whole lot harder in Breakbattle Academy.

"Let's check out the *battlefields*," Zachary finally said. "I heard the gyms are state of the art and stuff. All the best equipment."

The five of us took off to explore the rest of the school. We went into the gym, indoor swimming pool, and checked out the tracks and I figured out right away that state of the art was underselling it. No expense had been spared. Breakbattle boasted sleek courts, an Olympic-size pool, and nothing was worn or out of date. Everything was ready for the battles that would come in the new school year.

We did a lap around the grounds and then came back to meet up with Cameron and Santiago.

"We have half an hour until lunch," said Cameron. "We'll hang out and answer your questions and then you'll meet up with your folks."

That was fine with me. I still had a lot of questions. We followed the two inside to an empty classroom.

"This is a D classroom," Cameron said. "It should be reason enough to place higher."

I looked around. The class resembled the ones I had seen on television and in movies. Rows of chairs lined up before a simple brown desk and a whiteboard. "If this is considered bad, what are the F classrooms like?" I asked.

Cameron peered at me over his shoulder. "You should hope you don't find out."

"Forget the F Class," Zach said as he grabbed a seat. "What are the Elite classrooms like?"

"You should hope you do find out." Cameron hopped onto the desk next to his friend. "Alright, you've got questions, we'll answer, but first, tell us who you are and what class you think you'll get into."

Zach's hand shot into the air. "Zachary Fields. My family owns Fields Hospitals. All As in science—bio and chem—so I'm getting into the Elite Class."

Cameron lifted his foot onto the desk and draped his arm over his knee. He was the picture of poised and I couldn't take my eyes off of him. Not just because he was handsome, but because he had the look of someone who had everything come easy to him in life. He had yet to face a problem he couldn't handle or an obstacle he couldn't overcome. It was funny that in twenty-six countries and cultures, that look of self-confidence was the same.

"It's not just about the grades," said Cameron. "At our level, you have to kick ass on the court too."

Zachary didn't lose his grin. "I was the captain of my baseball team too. Trust me, I'm getting in."

"Nice." Cameron's eyes darted in my direction. "You."

"I think—"

He held up a hand. "Not you, Manning. I want to hear from Moon. Where does the son of the tech mogul, record producer, television reporter, CEO, and therapist think he is going?"

Son of the who now? I twisted around in my seat, facing Adam. *How many parents does he have?*

Adam's signature smile hung on his lips. "My mom and dads don't care where I go, but I'm alright with English and can hold my own in the water. I'd say A Class."

A snort sounded to my right. "Alright with English? Hold your own in the water?" Owen repeated. "Dude, you won the state essay contest three years in a row and came in second behind Reed in last year's swim meet, and that was only by half of a second. You're Elite, for sure."

I glanced back at Adam, seeing the chill, jovial guy in a new light.

"I wouldn't be so sure," Cameron's voice cut in smoothly. "The Elites don't do second place, but I would like to meet this Reed guy."

Adam's tone didn't change. "You'll get your chance. I saw him in the auditorium. He's here too."

"Then, you'll have another chance to prove you're better than him."

Adam's reply was immediate. "I'm not better than him or anyone else."

"Then, you're not Elite."

I stiffened even though I wasn't part of the conversation. You could cut the tension in the air, and despite Adam's neutral expression, I sensed there was a history between him and Cam.

"Manning."

I jumped.

"It's your turn. Tell us who you are and where you want to go."

I twisted around to face the pair. Cameron was smiling, but Santiago looked like he was seconds away from putting his head on the desk and going to sleep.

"Alright." I got to my feet and cleared my throat. "My name is Zeke Manning. My mom is a writer—"

"What does she write?"

"She writes..." The words stuck in my throat when I turned to see who spoke.

It was the eyes that struck me. A shocking blue that invoked visions of freshly skimmed swimming pools and powder blue jelly beans. They couldn't be his real eye color, but as I traced his face, I could see it suited him. Conventional was a word I doubt people used to describe this boy.

He wore a skin-tight newsprint suit and leather shoes that gleamed. His olive-toned chest peeked through his open collar, and his thick, black hair was gelled back on the sides while the top hung down to his eyes. I didn't know how it was possible that I hadn't noticed him before, but he was all I could see now.

"What does she write?" he repeated, jarring me out of my fog.

"She writes women's fiction."

"Anything we would have heard about?"

I shrugged. "Do you guys read women's fiction?"

I got a round of headshakes. "Then, no. Probably not. Anyway—"

"What about your dad?"

I stiffened.

I hated that question. I hated the way it followed me around my whole life. How it entered almost every single conversation I had. Four harmless words on their own, but together, they ripped me apart, because every time I had to say four words in reply.

"My dad is dead."

"Oh. Sorry."

I didn't have trouble looking away from him then. I shifted back to Cameron. "My mom is a writer and we just moved back into town. Before that, we traveled and she homeschooled me."

"This your first time in a real school?"

"Yes. We've been on the road since I was a baby."

"How many countries have you been to?"

"Twenty-six."

A low whistle cut through the silence. I could hear murmurs of appreciation, but it was Cameron's response that interested me. The smile melted away as his expression turned assessing.

"You know any other languages?" he asked.

"I'm fluent in three, not including English."

"Which ones?"

"Spanish, French, and Afrikaans."

"So language, geography, and world history. Are those your subjects?"

"No. I'm good at those, but math is my subject."

Cameron lifted a brow. "You think so?"

"I know so," I replied without skipping a beat. "I never had classmates to compare myself to, but... math is my subject."

Cameron cut eyes to Santiago and that made me turn my attention to him. The guy did not look bored now. "Let's see if that's true," said Cameron.

"What do you—"

Santiago climbed off the desk as if that was his cue. I watched in confusion as he walked up to the whiteboard and picked up a marker.

"If you're that good," said Santiago, "then you'll have no problem answering this." He scribbled out a problem as he spoke. "If x is more than zero, but less than pi over two. What is this expression equal to?"

Santiago wrote out an equation loaded with sines and cosines and all of them squared. My mind shot into gear before he wrote the last minus. I may not have known how to act like a boy or go to a regular school, but I knew this.

Trigonometry equations flashed across my vision, whirling and zipping through my mind's eye as the numbers formed, multiplied, canceled themselves out, and then finally revealed their answer to me.

Santiago turned away from the board, holding out the marker. "You can work out the problem, but you can't look up anything—"

"The answer is two."

He stopped. "What?"

"I said the answer is two."

Santiago looked between me and the board. "But you didn't—" A scowl twisted his face. "You can't just guess."

"I didn't guess. The square root of the value squared will cancel out and it will become the original value. The problem then becomes sine x over sine x plus cosine x over cosine x. That is one plus one, which equals two. The answer is two."

Santiago said nothing. The disinterest in his gaze was long gone and replaced with an intensity that pierced through me. I'm not sure how, but it felt like I had done something wrong.

"Damn," Zachary said. "I don't know what the hell he's talking about, but it sounded good. Is he right?"

"Well, Santi," Adam spoke up when he didn't answer. "Is he right?"

"He's right," Cameron said smoothly. He peered at his friend. "Impressive, wouldn't you say, Santi? Not even you got that problem right on the first try and he calculated it in his head."

"Shut up," Santiago snapped. "He probably answered it before. I'll give him another one."

"No need." Cameron turned back to me. "You good at sports?"

"I was homeschooled," I said simply. "I didn't have PE class."

"Shame, but I'd like to see you pull something out in the trials. We don't have a multilingual or anyone else as good at math as Santi. We could use you in the Elite Class."

"Use me?" My brows drew together. "But you're going to be sophomores. We wouldn't be in the same class."

"Of course we'll be in the same class. Us Elites stick together."

I picked up something belying those words. Between Cameron's grin and Santi's glare, I knew something had changed, but I didn't know what.

"Does that include the girl Elite Class?" The question was out of my mouth before I could stop it. "Do you stick with them?"

"Yes," he replied. There was no hesitation.

"If you feel that way, why is it like this? Why are the boys and girls in separate classes and only allowed to mix at meal times?"

"Yeah. Why is that?" Owen piped up. "It straight up sucks. What do they think we're going to do?"

"It's not about sex," Cameron said bluntly. "The school used to be mixed. Everything was fine for a while, but it became obvious it wasn't going to work."

"Why?" I pressed. I was different from my mother in many ways, but while the question of the gender separation disgusted her, it had defined me. It had brought me here, forced me into this role, and burned beneath the decisions I would have to make and the things that I would have to do.

I balled my fists behind my back. My heart beat against my chest, pumping blood that boiled beneath my skin. Everything had changed that day. One moment I had been Zela Manning—a content fifteen-year-old girl who was looking forward to going to high school with her cousin.

But then he changed everything and now I won't be Zela Manning for a long time... maybe never again.

"Because of the battle system," Cameron continued, unaware of the war raging inside of me. "The point of the system is to make sure the best rise to the top and the others stay where they belong, but things got out of hand. Some of the guys saw the girls as easy targets so they exclusively challenged them to battles over and over again until they won. One year, there was a girl in the B Class who ended up having over ten battles a week because the guys singled her out.

"She had excellent grades but wasn't as good at sports, so they figured they would just keep challenging her until one of them managed to beat her at the academic test. She couldn't say no without hurting her grade, but all the battles, extra tests, and constant running around wore her down. Her schoolwork started slipping, and by the end of the semester, she was a mess."

The room was deadly silent as Cameron revealed the awful tale.

"She finally lost and ended up in the D Class. She wasn't the only one. When the year ended, there were no girls in the Elite or A Class, and only two in the B Class. The girl's parents got involved—both of them high-priced lawyers—and they threatened to sue the school for allowing their daughter to be bullied and harassed. The parents of the other girls promised to join in on the suit if Breakbattle didn't do something about it.

"Breakbattle encourages competition, but not even they could defend what the boys were doing. Their solution to stop the targeting was to separate the classes. People are pissed about it, but no one else has come up with a better solution."

"I have one," I replied. "The school could cap the number of battles a student can be in each semester and, oh yeah, people can stop being assholes."

A whoop sounded behind me. "I'm with Zeke," Zachary cried. "Bring the girls back."

Zachary kicked off a round of applause. Over the din, Cameron kept his attention fixed on me.

"Interesting idea, Manning. You should take it up with the vice principal."

"Maybe I will." After a few seconds, I broke our gaze and retook my seat.

"Keep the introductions going," said Cameron, but I could still feel his eyes boring into me as another boy spoke up.

Chapter Three

"Today was..."

Adam laughed. "You don't have to say. I know."

The two of us were back in our dorm room, getting ready for the opening dinner. I said my goodbyes to Mom, Jordan, and Aunt Bev at lunch, but unlucky for me, the affable Adam rolled up and introduced himself to my family as my new friend and roommate.

Jordan and Aunt Bev took one look at him and the look in their eyes said it all. I was in for it the moment he left.

"Zee, you better *behave* yourself," Auntie hissed.

I flushed hotly. "What's that supposed to mean? I'm not going to do anything."

"You better not. You keep those drawers on and that chest wrapped up, young lady." She made sure her voice didn't carry, but I was straight up mortified nonetheless.

"Honestly, Beverly," Mom cut in, rising to my defense. "This is not about boys. This is about enacting change and tearing down a discriminatory system."

"That's what it'll be about until she waddles home pregnant."

I edged away from them, praying no one figured out I was with those people. I thought I couldn't be more embarrassed until Jordan came after me.

"Forget my mom. That Adam guy is hot as hell. If you don't climb that like a tree, I'll never forgive you."

"I'm not climbing anything!"

She rose up, looking over my head. "Can I have him, then? I'm not finding anything like that in Chesterfield High."

I grabbed her shoulders and spun her around. "Goodbye, Jordan. Take your mother and your aunt and go."

Laughing, she skipped away and dragged our arguing mothers out. I felt a moment of relief when they were gone, but only for a moment. That peace was soon broken by the realization that I was on my own in a school full of boys with everything to lose.

I pushed my anxiety down and locked it away as I straightened my bow tie. I looked pretty good. Jordan had hooked me up with dark blue pants and a matching shirt and tie. Adam was already dressed and waiting by the door. He looked great in black slacks and a striped green shirt. His hair he allowed to do what it wanted and the curls flopped down in front of his eyes.

"Adam."

"What's up?"

"I want to apologize for my family."

"What? Why? They were nice."

I pulled my head out of the wardrobe and gave him a look. "Trust me. I promise I'll never subject you to them again."

He threw his head back, laughing. "You're a weird guy, but I like you. How about I even the score and introduce you to my mother? She'll be at the dinner tonight."

"Really? Okay, cool."

I finished getting dressed and we left. I snuck glances at Adam while we headed down the stairs.

"So," I began. "I heard you say earlier about your mom and dads—plural."

"Yes, plural," he said without breaking his stride. "I've got four dads."

"Um... how?"

He chuckled. "They're my mom's boyfriends. She's been with them since I was a baby, so I call them all Dad."

"Oh. Okay." I fell quiet. For a while, all you could hear was the echo of shoes on the concrete steps.

"Thank you."

I raised my head. "Thank you? For what?"

"For restraining yourself and not saying it's weird or gross. I've heard it all since I was a kid."

"I would never say that. I don't think it either."

"Sure."

"I'm serious." I grabbed his arm and pulled him up short, halting on the third-floor landing. "I don't think it's weird. I've lived in a lot of places and experienced many cultures. I've met women with multiple partners. Guys with multiple partners too. We're all just living our lives. Oooh." I gave him a little shake. "I even lived in this one village where women are expected to raise their children with their brothers."

He goggled at me. "Have children with their brothers?"

"No, they don't reproduce with them. They go out, find some guy to lend his DNA and then when they get pregnant, they come back home and their brother or brothers will act as the children's father. The idea is that the best people to raise a family with is your family." I lifted my shoulders. "I've seen it all, man. There are plenty of families out there and I don't judge."

He cracked a smile. "You're alright, Zeke Manning."

"It's true, I am."

Laughing, we picked up our feet and kept going. I made it to the bottom floor before I opened my mouth again. "Do you mind if I ask another question?"

"Shoot."

"You said they've been with your mom since you were a baby. What about your biological father?"

I braced myself for Adam to tell me to go to hell. I knew it was a personal question, but I couldn't hold it back. There was a need in me that had existed my whole life. Something I could never talk about with Mom. If there was a chance that he knew what I had gone through, I needed to know. I needed someone to share it with.

"He died before I was born." I saw him look at me out of the corner of my eye. "And your dad..."

"I never knew him either." The words were hard to say, but I forced them out. "He left before I was born too. Told my mom he wanted nothing to do with me and wouldn't pay a cent of child support. Then when I was six, she told me he died."

"I'm sorry."

"It's okay. It was a long time ago."

We were quiet for a moment until Adam broke the silence.

He nudged my arm. "Tell me more about the places you've been. Where was that village you were talking about?"

"That was in..."

We chatted as we passed through the halls for the dining room. The doors were open when we arrived and I almost stopped in the entrance, not believing what I was seeing. The plain white and gray space I ate in earlier that day was transformed. The lunch benches had been swapped out for circular tables covered with reddish-gold linens. My new classmates weaved through the party dressed in their finest.

Adam and I moved over to the buffet line and loaded up a plate with finger foods. We would have a formal sit-down dinner later, but first, we were expected to mingle.

"I'm going to find my mom," Adam said as he left the buffet. "You coming with?"

"I'll—" Something caught my eye and I stopped. "I'll catch up to you."

Adam went on while I veered off. Cameron gestured to me again, inviting me over to the group assembled near the head table. There were five of them and none had changed their clothes. The letter E blazed proudly on their chest. All eyes turned on me as I drew near and Cameron stepped out of the pack.

"This is the guy I was telling you about." He put his arm around my shoulder and held me to his side like he thought I was going to run away. "A potential Elite."

Santi scoffed. "He answered one question, Cam, and he admitted he sucks at sports. Don't put the E on his blazer just yet."

I bristled. I didn't like Cameron showing me off like his newest prize, but I wasn't cool with Santiago underestimating me either. "If I want that E on my blazer, I'll get it."

Cameron shook me. "I like that attitude, Manning. That's what separates the Elites from the As. Your boy Moon has the ability, but he doesn't have the hunger. He's not willing to do whatever it takes, but if you want to be on top, you have to blow past the boundaries."

The guys before me inclined their heads, agreeing as one. A niggle of unease unfurled in my gut as Cameron dropped his arm and moved in front of them, facing me.

"Do you understand what I'm saying, Manning?"

The dim lights from the artificial candles flickered in his eyes. It enhanced the overwhelming sense I've had since I met him—the feeling that he was seeing right through me.

"Yes," I rasped. "I understand."

His smile told me I had said the right thing. "Boys, what do you think?"

"We need a multilingual." I didn't know the short, bespectacled guy who spoke, but Argyle had introduced him that day as Heath Dowell. "But Santi is right. Let's see how he does on the first day of the trials."

Cameron inclined his head. "Fair enough."

Just like that, he turned his back on me. I was dismissed.

I wandered away from the group in search of Adam.

What was that about? It was like I was a fatted calf up for auction. Or like they were approving me for acceptance into their class, but it wasn't like they decided who became Elite. How I scored on the placement test and in the trials did.

My mind spun with questions, but no answers. Maybe those dudes were just weirdos. It would explain Santi looking at me like I personally offended him for answering a math question, and Cameron going on about being better than everyone. Definitely weirdos.

"—Mom, come on."

The low whine caught my notice. I recognized that voice.

"Everyone is looking."

I slipped through two suit-clad boys and found Adam standing near the drinks table in the clutches of a stunningly beautiful woman. Wavy, chestnut hair framed impossibly smooth skin and fell across Adam's face as she attacked him with kisses.

"What?" she asked. "You don't want your friends to know how much your momma loves you?"

Adam spotted me through the curtain of her hair and mouthed one word, "Help."

I stifled a giggle as I strode up to the pair.

"Mom, this is my friend Zeke."

His mother released him and turned to face me. My eyes flicked to her swelling abdomen. She was pregnant.

"Nice to meet you, Zeke. You can call me Miss Val. I'm the school therapist. Are you looking forward to the coming school year?"

I shook her outstretched hand. "Yes and no."

"No?"

"I'm a little worried about the battles and stuff."

"Oh, yes, of course. Most new students feel some anxiety about it but know that you can talk to me whenever you need. You don't have to wait for our appointments."

"Appointments." I backed away slightly. "What appointments?"

Adam spoke up. "All students have to meet with Mom at least twice a semester."

"We do?" I swung back to Miss Val. "Why?"

"Just to make sure you're coping. The battle system adds more tests and training to an already heavy workload. It's important to check in."

I nodded. That made sense.

Val's eyes drifted over my shoulder. "Sorry. Will you excuse me? One of my colleagues is calling me over."

I waved goodbye as she strode away. "Wow. Your mom is so—"

"Young," he finished.

"Pretty. I swear I was going to say pretty." I glanced at her retreating back. "But yeah, she does look young. Do we really have to meet with her twice a semester? You too?"

"Not me. She's my mom. Instead, they're sending me to the therapist for the girls, and yes, it's mandatory after— after what happened."

Something in his voice made me look at him. "What? Tell me."

He let out a breath. "You remember what Cameron said today about the girl who was targeted by the boys until they knocked her down to the D Class?"

"Yes. What about her?"

"Well, he left out part of the story. That girl... committed suicide."

My plate almost slipped from my fingers. "She what?"

"It was too much. She worked so hard and they came after her relentlessly until they took it all away." He sighed. "My mom has worked here for years. She does her best to make sure the students are okay, but this is a tough place. The competition is brutal and some people will do anything to get on top."

My eyes drifted to the five boys in the corner sporting Es on their chest.

"It might get intense, but we'll have each other's backs." He clapped me on the shoulder. "Right?"

"Yes, we will," I said softly. "I can handle whatever Break-battle throws at me. I have to."

BEEP! BEEP! BEEP!

Groaning, I cracked an eye open and glared at the offending thing. My hand shot out of the covers and whacked the snooze button.

"Don't think about going back to sleep," a voice said just as I closed my eyes. "We can't miss our first trial."

"Why do we have to go so early?" I heaved myself up, blinking blearily. "We can't perform our best if we're half—" Adam came into focus.

"Ahhhh!"

"Ah!" He leaped a foot in the air, whipping around. "What?! What is it?!"

"What is it?! Why are you naked?!"

Adam stood at the foot of his bed wearing nothing but tight, blue briefs and a look on his face like I was insane. "That's why you yelled? You scared me half to death, dude."

"I-I'm sorry. I just..." I sunk down, letting the covers ride up over my face. "I wasn't expecting to see your milk-pale thighs first thing in the morning."

He burst out laughing. "Shut up, Zeke."

I hid until I heard the bathroom door close and the shower turn on. Adam was clearly comfortable with his new roommate and I wished I could feel the same. At home, I slept in loose cotton nighties, no bra, and fuzzy socks. That wasn't an option last night. I didn't take off my bindings for fear Adam would wake up in the middle of the night, stumble to the bathroom, and see more mounds under my blankets than there should be. If this week was a taste of what was to come, it would be a long four years.

Adam came out of the bathroom a little while later and then I got ready. In half an hour, we were out the door and headed to breakfast.

"I hope I didn't freak you out last night," Adam said as we tromped down the stairs. "Becca Taylor's story is sad, but the school split the classes and hired people like my mom to make sure these things don't happen again."

"It is sad, and I can even understand why they chose to split the classes, but I wonder why they didn't change the battle system instead. Or get rid of it entirely."

"They're not going to do that. They believe in it and they want to prove that it's the best way to educate students. Mom has tried many times to get the principal and vice principal to make changes, but every student that graduates and becomes a big success just proves to them that Breakbattle is doing something right."

I glanced at him in surprise. "Do you not like the system?"

"I've heard too much from my mom and dads to think it's perfect, but all of my friends are here and— I'd just rather be here than a local high school."

I caught that slipup, but I didn't push it. We had only known each other for a day. I'd give it more time before I tried to pry secrets out of him, but I would pump him for something else.

"Since you're my well of information," I said as we walked into the cafeteria. "Tell me how I missed that this school is for rich kids. My jaw was on the floor yesterday when the other guys were introducing themselves and saying who their parents were."

"It's not, but—"

"Totally ridiculous." A sharp voice floated over the noise and reached our ears.

There was one stark difference about the cafeteria since the day before, and they were wearing plaid skirts and filling the room with the heady scent of perfumes.

A group of girls were gathered by the trays. In the center was a girl with sandy hair and a blue top. "Mom and Dad don't want to send me to a school out of state, but this place is crazy."

I glanced up at Adam when he didn't go on, but his eyes weren't on me. "Hey, Melody."

The girl stopped talking and turned at his voice. "Oh, hey." She tilted her head, peering at him. "It's Aaron, right?"

"Adam."

She snapped her fingers. "That's it." She broke away from her group and sauntered up to my suddenly silent friend. I looked her up and down. It was no wonder he was struck dumb. She was the kind of beautiful that people wrote songs about. Her hips even swayed as she moved. "I forgot you were coming here."

"Uh-huh."

Melody placed her hand on his arm and Adam went visibly stiff. "Can you believe this place? Separating us because they think we can't handle the boys. Not to mention making us participate in their stupid battle thing in the first place. I was just talking with my friends. I may have to go to school here, but I don't have to put up with this shit. We're going to do something about it."

"Okay."

A smile lit her face. "You'll help us, won't you?"

Adam didn't try to speak this time. He just nodded so hard I thought his head would pop off.

"You're sweet." She turned and walked off, waving her fingers as she went. "Bye."

I stared at Adam with huge eyes. I didn't bother to leave the grin off my face and he winced when he finally looked at me. "Don't say it."

"Don't say what?" I teased. "You were not saying plenty enough for the both of us."

He groaned. "I know. I act like a total idiot around her." Adam moved up to the line. "Let's change the subject. What were we talking about before? Oh yeah. School for the rich." He picked up two trays and handed one to me. "It's not, but it seems that way since most of the kids from my town end up here."

My brows crawled up my forehead. "Your town? Does that mean that you're...?"

"Rich?" He grinned, recovering quick. "Me. No. But my dads. Filthy."

I hummed. "You guys like big families. Do you have room for me?"

Adam guffawed. "You're so weird, Zeke, but I don't think I'd mind you as a brother."

His laughter pulled a chuckle out of me. We might have known each other for only a day, but at that moment, I knew we were friends.

We went down the line and the lunch lady piled a breakfast burrito, dry cereal, an apple, and a carton of milk on to our plates. It was still pretty early, so we sat down to an empty table and dug in as the other students trickled in.

"So who do you know from your old school?" I asked. "Did you go to school with all the guys in our group?"

"Not all of them. Owen, Zachary, Justin, and"—he jerked his chin toward the door—"Landon Foster."

I spun around before the last name was out of his mouth. Landon Foster was the pale-blue-eyed boy that asked me about my mother. My breath caught once more when I saw him.

He was wearing another show-stopping outfit. Ripped black jeans covered his legs up the thigh where it disappeared beneath a large, stringy sweater. That wasn't as surprising as the oversized scarf that hung down so low it almost touched the floor.

"Does he always dress like that?" I asked, eyes glued on him.

"Yes. His dad is a fashion designer. You should have seen him in middle school. He came to school every day in outfits that cost enough to feed a family of five."

As if he sensed us talking about him, his head shot up and he looked me right in the eye.

"*Eep.*" I made a choked noise and breathing only got harder when Landon took his tray and walked right up to us.

"Sup, Moon. You feeling generous?"

"It's all yours." Adam handed over his apple.

"Thanks. She wouldn't give me more."

I sat stiff as a board, my lips glued shut. *What is wrong with me? Say something. Do something.*

"Wrestling is the first trial," Adam went on. "You ready?"

"Course I'm ready. I'm getting into the Elite Class or I'm dropping out, but it won't come to that." Landon clapped his hand on my shoulder and I jerked, almost toppling out of my seat. "Sorry about that thing with your dad yesterday. Didn't know."

"I-it's okay," I croaked.

His eyes flicked down to my plate. "Are you going to eat that?"

It took me a second to connect that he was talking about my apple. I was going to eat it, but inexplicably, my hand closed around it and offered it up.

"Thanks, man." He backed away. "See you guys on the mat."

I watched him until he found an empty table and plopped down, munching on my apple.

"He's got a thing for apples," Adam explained, "and I hate them so he's been taking them off my hands since elementary school."

"What were you guys talking about? Is he a wrestler?" I tried to keep the surprise out of my voice, but I didn't do a great job. A model I would believe, but a wrestler?

"Oh yeah. He won the regional tournament last year, and like he said, he's gunning for the Elite Class." He shrugged. "He'll probably get in too. Everyone underestimates him because of the clothes and colored contacts, but he's a straight-A student and slippery on the mat. You think you've got him and the next thing you know, he's on top of you and the ref is calling it."

"Sounds like you speak from experience."

Adam tore a bite out of his burrito before continuing. "I do. The guy beat me every time I went up against him in gym class, but wrestling is not my sport. I'm a swimmer."

"Right." I picked up my own food and peeled off the foil. "You're so good, Owen says you're destined for the top class."

"Don't know about that. It depends on how I do in the swimming trial against... him."

Once again, I looked up... and the burrito slipped through my fingers as my eyes landed on the boys. The two of them strolled up to the lunch line. Their clothes might have been painfully plain in comparison to Landon, but their faces had obviously been sculpted by the same angelic hands.

"The shorter guy is Cole Reed." Adam's voice sounded far away. "Swimmer. Next to him is his friend Michael Young. Michael is a runner."

That made perfect sense. Michael was as tall as he was lithe. His body was built for speed. Sharp cheekbones and an angular face drew my attention to those serious brown eyes. There was no denying he was handsome.

Then there was Adam's competition. Cole was smoother while his friend was sharp. Soft-looking cheeks, clean-shaven, and his hair cut close to the scalp. He fashioned himself to slide effortlessly through the water.

Adam was still speaking. "They're both going after the Elite spots t—"

"Why is everyone at this school gorgeous?"

"What?"

I blinked. "What?"

Did I just say that out loud?

Adam squinted at me. "What did you say?"

"I-I didn't say anything," I cried. "What did you say?"

"I said they want to be Elite," he repeated slowly. "Then you said something about everyone in the school is—"

"Talented!" I burst out. "You guys got skills. You'll all be Elite! Ha. Haha!" I laughed wildly and a bit too loudly if the looks people were throwing me were anything to go by.

"But... only ten guys can be in the Elite Class. You know that."

"That's right."

"Right." Shaking his head, Adam picked up his burrito and kept eating. He didn't have to say it. I could practically hear "you're so weird," go through his mind.

I glanced away, looking back toward Michael and Cole just as the cafeteria doors opened. A group entered the room—laughing and carrying on loud enough that every eye turned to them, but that wasn't what held me fast.

There were half a dozen girls orbiting around him, moving in step with him as he crossed over to the food. My gaze was glued to him and the others faded in my vision. I started at the top of his spiky, brownish-blond hair and then moved down over his piercing eyes, his upturned nose, and full lips. The guys at this school were gorgeous, but this one was in a league of his own.

"That's Derek Grayson," Adam supplied. "Another guy from my town."

"Derek Grayson." My tongue cradled the letters as they strung together and fell from my lips.

"He's right there with Landon. He's told everyone that if he doesn't get into the Elite Class, he is transferring to another school."

I listened with half an ear. Derek was laughing about something one of the girls said. Not a soft, polite laugh, but one that wracked his body and transformed his face. He took his tray and weaved through the room for an empty table.

In the next breath, I was on my feet. Time slowed down as Derek pulled out a chair and plopped down. He reached for his apple first. Long, slender fingers wrapped around the red skin and brought it to his pale pink lips. He took a bite, tearing off a chunk with perfect teeth and beads of juice squirted onto his mouth and traveled down his chin.

I could see it all clearly because he was coming closer.

No, wait. It was me who was closing the distance between us. My feet had carried me over to Derek Grayson and the sound of Adam calling me faded in the background.

He looked up at me when my hand closed over the seat. My heart rocketed in my chest as I lowered myself next to him. It pounded in my ears.

My jaw worked, opening and closing, as I tried to speak. A tiny wrinkle appeared between his brows as he watched me. "Hi, D-Derek," I forced out. "I'm—"

"What the fuck are you doing?"

I froze. *What did he just say?*

"Who said you could sit here?"

"I was— I was just—"

"I don't know you."

"I just wanted to talk to you."

"Why would I want to talk to you?"

"Uhh. Why not?"

"Excuse me? You all think you own me or something because you saw my face in a magazine." Derek's charming smile was gone. Irritation etched into the lines of his handsome face and I cringed before it. "I'm not signing your chest, fanboy." His voice was rising and drawing the attention of the entire school and my cheeks flushed hot. "And you're not getting a selfie! Move the hell on before you piss me off!"

I shot out of the chair so fast it toppled over. The sound of the crash was covered by uproarious laughter. People pointed and howled at me as I raced out of the room.

Tearing through the halls, the smiling faces of Breakbattle's success stories blurred in the wake of my stinging tears. I burst out onto the lawn and ran with no thought to where I was going.

I LEANED AGAINST THE wall. The brick scraped against my back, but I didn't care. It wasn't as annoying as the boys posted up a few feet away, looking over at me every now and then to make sure I knew they were talking about me. We were minutes away from our very first trial, but my breakfast teardown was more interesting.

"Yo, Zeke!" I tore my eyes away to see Adam jogging up to me. "There you are. I've been looking all over for you."

"You didn't have to do that," I mumbled.

"Yes, I did. You—" Adam frowned. "Hey. Were you crying?"

I ducked my head as I roughly rubbed my eyes. "No. It's just allergies."

"Sure it is." A hand grasped my shoulder. "Look, I'm sorry about breakfast. That wasn't cool, but he's Derek Grayson. His mother is that famous actress, Naomi Grayson, and he played in a few of her movies when he was little. He's used to people following him around, sneaking shots, begging for autographs, and getting into his face all the time. The guy doesn't trust anyone he doesn't know, especially after..." Adam trailed off. "I'm just saying that it wasn't about you. He would have blown up on anyone."

"It's okay, Adam. Really, it is." I lifted my head to let him see my smile. "I just want to focus on the trial." I sighed. "Although, I've never wrestled in my life so I'm most likely going to be humiliated twice today."

Adam threw his arm over my shoulder and led me off. "It won't be so bad. The key is to remain on the offensive and rely on your strengths. What do you have going for you that your opponent doesn't?"

"Ignorance," I muttered under my breath. I appreciated Adam's support, but this was going to be a total disaster.

The door flew open just as we joined the line. I knew the man who stepped outside. He was one of the coaches who introduced himself at the opening ceremony. Breakbattle had five coaches. This one in particular was Coach Franklin. He had on a cap, but underneath his head was shiny smooth. The man had muscles on his muscles and the clear, no-nonsense glint in his eyes told of his discipline.

"Good morning, gentlemen."

"Morning, Coach."

"Today is your first trial. I will explain how it's going to work, so listen up. You will enter the gym, get changed, and then form four lines in front of the scales. After you're weighed, you will be matched up with your opponent."

Coach didn't yell or raise his voice, but his instructions carried over the heads of the boys to where I was standing next to Adam, fighting the urge to flee.

"These matches are about more than just winning. I am evaluating your stamina, ability to think on your feet, conduct, and overall skill. Win or lose, each student will receive a score that will contribute to your final grade at the end of the week. A low score on this trial could be the difference from getting into the class you want, so take this seriously. Any questions?"

My hand shot up in the air.

"Yes. You at the back."

"Coach, what if you have never wrestled before?"

His expression remained blank. "Then, your score will reflect your inexperience."

"But can't we practice first? Learn the rules?"

"No."

I bit back a scowl. "That's not fair."

"Life isn't fair, boy." Coach stepped to the side. "Now, go in and get changed."

The boys streamed past him into the gym. Three boxes were waiting for us in the middle of the polished floors and the guys didn't waste time in searching out their sizes, grabbing a uniform, and heading for the locker room. When it was Adam's turn, he reached into the medium box and held up the uniform.

My eyes bugged out. "What the heck is that!? A string bikini?"

He laughed. "They prefer singlet."

Whatever they called it, I could not wear that. There was barely any cover over the chest and if I was going to be rolling and wrestling on the mat, I wasn't trusting my fate to my bindings.

I moved over to the small sizes and rifled around for one with a lot more fabric.

Nothing. There has to be another—

I lifted my head and my eyes lit upon more boxes against the back wall. Small, medium, and large were scrawled on their sides.

Must be more in there.

I jogged over and pulled open the box. I pulled one out and deflated with relief. It was exactly what I was looking for. This singlet would cover my chest, and as long as I wore it over my white tee, no one would see my wrappings.

I threw the uniform over my shoulder and walked over to Adam. He wasn't alone. Justin, Owen, and Zachary had joined him and all four of them were openly staring at me.

My smile dimmed. "What? What is it?"

Owen made a face. "Zeke, what are you doing with that? That's the girls' uniform."

"It is?" Heat flooded my cheeks. Of course, it is. That's why it's perfect for a *girl* in hiding. "Oh. I didn't know."

"Are you worried you're too small to fit into the boys'?" Zach bent down and pulled a singlet out of the box. "Because this one should fit."

I didn't reach for it. They were trying to help, but I could not wear that and I couldn't say why.

"Thanks, but I'll wear this anyway. It'll... fit me better."

Zach shrugged. "Whatever. Let's just get changed."

I followed the four of them in the direction of the locker room but veered off at the last second for the toilets. I was keeping my shirt and shorts on, but who knew if the other boys were. I was not ready to see manflesh.

I was the first one finished. When I came out, I saw Coach Franklin had set out the scales, so I walked up to one to wait. I expected Coach to say something about my outfit, but his face might have been etched in stone. He took one look at me and then went back to his clipboard.

The squeak of rubber against the maple flooring signaled the boys were emerging from the locker room. A shadow fell over me, but I took no notice until he spoke.

"Nice singlet."

I knew who it was before I turned around. Landon Foster's chest was the first thing to greet my eyes. Out of the suit and the baggy sweater, I saw instantly why it was a mistake to underestimate him. Those expensive clothes had been hiding a body that was all compact, lean muscle.

"You too," I said as I traveled up his chest to his face. He could have been making fun of me, but it was hard to tell. He looked as mildly blank as he did when I saw him that morning.

"The point is to start where you belong."

I blinked. "What?"

Landon lowered his head and looked me in the eye. "That's why Coach won't teach us or give us tips. It's why they didn't send out study guides to prepare us for the placement test. Whatever we can or cannot do right now will decide where we belong in Breakbattle, and if you end up on the bottom, you have to show you're willing to fight your way to the top. I am." I gulped as those pale blue eyes bore into me. "Are you?"

It took me a second to answer. "Is that your way of saying you won't go easy on me if we're paired up?"

He cracked a smile. "No. You're on the scrawny side, so I doubt we'll be matched up. That was me giving you the only tip you'll get this week. Consider it a thank you for the apple."

I glanced over Landon's shoulder just as Derek walked out of the locker room. Our eyes met almost instantly and his grin fled beneath his scowl. Somehow, I had made an enemy of him and all I had done was sit in a chair.

My stomach twisted into knots at the sight of that glare. I turned away from him and Landon without another word.

"Okay, boys," announced Coach. "Let's get started."

One after the other, we stepped onto the scale to let Coach weigh us and sort us into groups. Landon was correct about us not being in the same weight class and I wasn't mad about it. Let some other poor sap go up against a wrestling champion.

"Everyone take a seat," Coach ordered. "Michael Young and Adam Moon. You're up first."

I claimed a seat next to Owen to watch the match. Despite his broken arm, Owen had insisted on doing the trial.

"You heard Coach," he told us. "A zero could be the difference between the C Class and the D Class. I have to try."

At least he's done this before. I'm the one who has never seen a proper wrestling match, let alone been in one. I focused on Adam and Michael. *I'd better pay attention, then.*

The boys circled the mat. I could almost liken it to a dance. Smooth, measured movements perfectly in sync with each other. When Adam stepped, Michael stepped.

Interesting, I thought as I studied them. *They never—*

Michael lunged forward and the match began. I was riveted. Every takedown, escape, hold, and move I captured and stored away. By the time Adam pinned Michael to the mat and

Coach called it, I understood that it was about more than brute strength. It was about using your head.

If I end up on the bottom, I have to figure out a way to get to the top.

Thinking of Landon's advice pushed me to seek him out. I twisted around on the seat, looking for the smart-mouth with the jelly bean eyes, and that's when I saw them.

Cameron and Santiago were sitting at the top of the bleachers. I hadn't noticed them come in.

"Alright, next up!"

The next pair walked up to the mat as Adam claimed the seat next to me. The trials were underway.

Two at a time, the guys stepped up and wrestled it out. Some matches were a real display of talent and skill, and others were a cringey mess between two people who clearly didn't know what they were doing. As expected, Coach Franklin offered no help or advice except to step in if someone did something dangerous or against the rules. Otherwise, it was just him and his clipboard.

He wrote something down as Owen stumbled off the mat, cradling his bad arm. He lost, of course, but I was hoping Coach had thrown some points his way.

"Zeke Manning and Justin Samuels."

I had been keeping it together rather well, but the nerves set in the second I stood up. Justin sauntered onto the mat, looking relaxed in his spandex. That wasn't the look of someone who didn't know what they were doing.

As I placed my foot on the mat, something made me look to the top of the bleachers. Cameron and Santiago were still there, and their eyes were fixed on me.

"Ready for this, Manning?" Justin bounced on the balls of his feet, grinning broadly. "I won't go easy on you, homeschooler."

I cracked a smile. "Don't underestimate me, Samuels. I've eaten live bugs and walked over bridges made of twine and twigs. I'm not worried about you."

"Gentlemen." A sharp voice cut through our banter. "Save the conversation for when you're on your own time. Shake hands."

We came to the center, shook, and then squared up. Coach blew his whistle and we were off. Or I should say, I was off. I shot away when Justin lunged. If he got his hands on me, he'd take me down in a flailing heap and it would all be over. I needed more time to figure him out and his weaknesses—if he had any.

Justin backed off slightly, circling with me while I studied his every move and breath. Justin stepped to the side, crossing his left foot in front of his right. My eyes flicked down at the movement and the next thing I knew those legs were running at me.

Justin charged, hands out, and I quickly twisted away and bolted to the other side of the mat. A chorus of snickers went up behind me, but I ignored it.

He faced me again, this time looking irritated as we circled each other once more. The next time he lunged, I was ready. Justin went low, aiming for my legs. I shot to the side and grabbed him around the middle. I grunted, readying to flip him the way I saw Adam do. I lifted him up...

...and my knees buckled. We collapsed to the mat in a heap, Justin on top of me. He recovered quickly and scrambled to pin me down, but I bucked and knocked him off. I ran to the other side of the mat, but this time he followed me.

I twisted so he wasn't at my back and we did another little dance as we circled each other only a hair's length away.

My eyes flicked down to his legs again. Justin stepped forward and—

Now!

I dropped, thrust my foot through his crossed legs, and kicked out.

"Ahhh!"

Justin dropped to the mat with a smack and I leaped on top of him. My chest was in his face as I grasped both hands and pinned them down.

I had two seconds to ride the thrill of victory before Justin reared up. The room spun as I went flying, and suddenly, I was looking up at the ceiling. I bucked and wriggled, but Justin had me fast.

Coach blew sharply on his whistle. The match was over.

I lost.

"IT WASN'T THAT BAD."

I stopped flicking through channels long enough to give Adam a look. Our first day was over and the two of us were back in our dorm watching television. Adam was chill in a baggy shirt and a pair of boxers while I had on full pajamas.

"I lost, Adam. How can it not be that bad?"

"You heard Coach. He scores based on more than who wins or loses. You might have done well."

Groaning, I flopped back onto the couch. "But tomorrow is going to be even worse. We have the swimming trials."

"What's wrong with that?"

Everything was wrong with it. I might have gotten away with wearing a girl's singlet today, but it wasn't like I could wear a girl's bathing suit for the swimming trial. I couldn't step out of the locker room bare-chested. I couldn't wear the boys' swim briefs. I couldn't swim.

"I can't swim, Adam."

"Oh, man. You don't know how?"

I opened my mouth to correct him and stopped. *Actually, that's a great excuse. I'll still get a zero, but at least everyone will understand why I won't get in the water.*

"Yep," I said instead. "I never learned."

He kissed his teeth. "And they'll still flunk you on the trial. This is so messed up. I'd teach you, but there's not much we can do in one night."

"No, but it's cool of you to offer. Don't worry about me. Just focus on beating Cole Reed."

"I'm not thinking about him. As long as I do well enough to get into the A Cl—"

Ring. Ring. Ring.

I shook my head. "You're a popular guy, Moon. That's the third call you got in an hour."

He laughed. "I've got a lot of parents all stressing about me being away from home for the first time. Plus, my little brother and sisters can't sleep unless I tell them goodnight. Get used to hearing my phone ring."

I got up while Adam took the call. I left him to it while I climbed into bed and burrowed beneath the covers. I didn't have siblings who wanted to say goodnight to me, but I always had Jordan. I slipped my phone under the blanket and shot her a text.

Me: Totally bombed my first trial and pissed off the child of a famous movie star. How did your day go?

Jordan: Got stuck going car shopping with your mom. She totally made an employee cry when he called her honey.

Me: Sounds like Mom.

Jordan: She got that car for a wicked good price though. But what about you? Is it really going that bad?

Me: I don't know. We don't find out our scores until the last day, but having to keep my secret is already hurting me. I didn't come here to get into the Elite Class, but it would make my life easier if I did.

Jordan: Everything is going to be fine, cuz. You've got this.

I took a breath and let it out slowly. Jordan was right. Everything would be fine. No matter how I did on the trials, I knew I would ace the placement test. That should get me into the right dorm and with enough privileges to survive while I focused on what I really came here to do.

Me: Yes, it will. Nothing is going to stop me. Nite, cuz.
Jordan: Nite.

"Goodnight," I heard Adam say. "Love you, guys."

I stuck my hand out of the covers and flicked the lamp off at the same time as Adam. We said our goodnights through the darkness. I snuggled into my pillow, relaxing for the first time that day, and let sleep carry me off.

"TIME TO GET UP!"

The shout jerked me to consciousness. I tore my eyes open, but shadows played across my vision, moving unnaturally in the darkness.

What the hell was going—

My eyes adjusted. Standing over me were two masked figures.

I screamed.

"Shut up!"

A hand clapped over my mouth. I lashed out, swiping at their face, but the other person caught me midair. They yanked me up and wrenched my arm behind my back. I couldn't think to escape before my hands were tied. Muffled cries to my right told me it wasn't just me being attacked.

What's going on?! Who are these people? What do they want with us?

The hand disappeared from my mouth and I took my chance. "Help! Help! Someone hel— *Argh!*"

Something was stuffed through my lips, gagging me. I whipped my head around, glaring into the eyeholes of the mask. Those dark, shadowed pools were the last thing I saw before they covered my head.

"Let's go," a deep voice sounded. "They're waiting for us."

I fought, yelled, and struggled as I was lifted out of bed. I had no idea where they were taking me, but the echo of their thundering on the steps told me we were going down the stairs.

"Stop," a distant voice cried. *"Wait!"*

I struggled harder when the cool air of the night touched my skin. Why were we outside? Where were they taking us?!

My bare feet skittered over the grass. The sound merely a whisper compared to the roaring in my ear. I thought I knew fear. I thought nothing could compare to what I had gone through, but I was wrong.

The eerie silence of our captors terrified me more than anything. They didn't need to coordinate or figure out what they were going to do to us. This had been planned.

Awful scenarios went through my head, each more horrifying than the last. *Adam said his parents were insanely wealthy. What if this is a kidnapping and they only took me because I was there? What are they going to do to me?*

I was spiraling by the time we came to a stop. A cold sweat covered my trembling body, collecting beneath my many layers and soaking me through.

My captors set me down and I felt the soft earth beneath my knees. Suddenly, their hands disappeared.

"Thank you, gentlemen."

I froze. That voice. I knew that voice.

"You can remove their blindfolds."

The cover was whisked off my head. Time slowed as I took in what was before me. The lanterns cast their dim glow on the trees surrounding us, but their light was for the boulder and the boy sitting on top of it. We were in the woods and the person peering down at me, smiling that carefree smile, was Cameron Dupre.

I screamed at him. I raged and cursed and swore every filthy word I knew, and he heard none of it through my gag. Even so, I wasn't the only one making their anger known. Adam had been placed next to me, and as I looked around, I saw more boys had been taken.

Cameron held up a hand. "Settle down, guys. No one is going to hurt you. We brought you here for a reason, and trust me, you're going to want to hear what we have to say."

Cameron stood and jumped off the boulder. My futile cries died in my throat as uncertainty gripped me.

"This is not a prank or hazing," Cameron began. "This is an opportunity. An opportunity that I was given during my orientation week by the Elites that came before me, and one they were given by those who came before them."

Cameron stopped in front of me. He met my eyes, towering over me as my body went rigid.

"We've chosen you because you're the ten most likely candidates to enter the Elite Class. That is an honor on its own, but it's one that's given by test scores and grades. To truly be one of us—to be accepted as an Elite—it is us who will do the choosing."

Cameron seemed to be speaking to everyone, but for some reason, his eyes didn't stray from me. "We invited you out tonight to let you know what we're about. To show you what you can become. We'll be watching. We'll be assessing you. And we'll let you know where you truly stand when this week is over."

I swallowed hard as another smile twisted his lips. He looked into my eyes... then he snapped his fingers.

"Ungag them."

A hand crossed my vision and tugged the gag out of my mouth. I didn't hold back when it was gone.

"What the hell!" I spat. "Have you ever heard of a text? What kind of psychos would kidnap people from their beds?!"

The guys around me were saying much the same.

Cameron wasn't fazed. "It's tradition. New candidates are brought out here for a little chat. If you want to run off whining, go ahead. We won't stop you." He looked over my shoulder. "You can untie them."

Someone grabbed my hands and freed me. I turned around and met their faces as they pulled the masks off. It was Santiago and one of the guys I met at the dinner, Heath Dowell. I looked around at everyone in the group. It wasn't just Heath, Santiago, and Cameron. I recognized the two other Elite Class boys they were with at the dinner.

They went down the row, untying the other guys: Adam Moon, Zachary Fields, Landon Foster, Cole Reed, Michael Young, three guys I didn't know, and—

"I'm going to kill your ass, Cameron!" Derek shoved Heath out of the way and stalked toward the older boy. He stuck his face in his, eyes blazing. "What the fuck is wrong with you?!"

Cameron didn't flinch. "Try to keep up, Grayson. We told you why you're here. We're offering you acceptance into the Elites. Don't let that mouth ruin it."

Derek scoffed. "I'm getting into the Elite Class either way. You don't decide shit."

"I'm not talking about the class. It's one thing to wear the E on your chest. It's another to truly be one of us."

My brows snapped together. Was that why only five of the Elites were here instead of their whole class? Were they not a part of their little... club?

But why would they think we would want to be?

"Why do you want me?" I asked. "Why do you want any of us?"

Cameron stepped past Derek like he wasn't there. "I'll tell you. I'll tell you everything as long as one thing is very clear. Nothing you see or hear tonight is to leave these woods." His pleasant smile evaporated. Cameron scanned the group with a look in his eyes that made me take an involuntary step back. "I'm serious. If you rat us out, you'll regret it. So leave *now* if you don't want to be one of us."

"I'm out." One of the guys I didn't know threw up his hands. "I'll keep my mouth shut, but whatever this is, I'm not interested." He grabbed his friends' arms. "Parker. Jose. Let's get out of here." The three slowly backed away. When they saw no one was going to stop them, they turned and ran.

I glanced at Adam, eyes questioning, but he wasn't looking at me nor was he moving. He stood stock-still, gazing at Cam. Not even Derek moved, although he still looked like he wanted to knock Cameron's head off.

Maybe it was loyalty, or it could have been curiosity, either way, I didn't leave either. I turned and faced Cameron.

"Alright, we're staying," I announced. "Explain."

"Gladly." He gestured at the others. "Come closer."

Slowly, the other boys moved in until we formed a semicircle in front of him and the Elites. The lanterns cast shadows over their faces as Cameron began. "It all started twelve years ago with the scandal that took down Evergreen Academy. You know about it, of course."

To my surprise, Adam and the other boys nodded. "No," I spoke up. "I don't."

Cameron inclined his head. "Right, you wouldn't. Ask your boy, Adam, about it later. He knows all the details." He took his eyes off me and kept going. "Like I was saying, the scandal hit the media and everyone found out what was really going on at that school, but while some people bleated and moaned about how awful it was, the members of the Elite junior class at the time saw its genius. That was the year they formed the Network."

"The Network?" I repeated.

"That's right. If there is one truth in this world, it's that it's all about who you know. That matters almost as much as what you know or how talented you are. Connections, boys. That's what the Network offers you, and Breakbattle is the key."

I opened my mouth. I think I had a question, but it died on my lips. Cameron's soft voice had me spellbound. My eyes followed him as he moved through the semicircle.

"This school makes it easy for us. They sort the worthless from the gems. The Elite Class is the best of the best. The smartest, the fastest, the strongest, the ones that not only have the ability to be great but the willingness to crush those who stand in their way. The Founders saw this and realized what a waste it is to let them graduate and then scatter to the wind.

"We should be banding together. We should be helping each other on the way to"—Cameron paused in front of Michael and Cole—"the Olympics. There are members in the Network who have gone and came home with the gold. Wouldn't you like to meet them? Wouldn't you like their endorsements, their tips, their coaching?"

Cameron slid away before they could answer. "And you, Foster." Landon's pool water eyes met Cameron's steadily. "I know you have bigger aspirations than Daddy's fashion line or Mommy's cosmetic company. It's hard to go against your parents, but it becomes a bit easier when you have others backing you. We have college scouts in the Network, Foster. If you want to take your wrestling all the way, there are people who can get you there."

Adam was close enough that I felt him stiffen when Cameron came to him. "Moon," he began. "I didn't want you. I didn't think you had what it took until I saw you go up against Young. There is a killer instinct somewhere beneath that toothy grin, and if you use it, you'll find yourself in the right position to make the connections that will help you when you take over Shea Industries. It's a big job running a billion-dollar company. I know you don't want to let one dad down, let alone all of them."

I sensed Adam getting tense. Taking the heat off him, I blurted, "What about me? What is your little club supposed to do for me and why would you want me in it anyway?" Cameron turned piercing eyes on me. "I lost today's trial and none of you know me."

He inclined his head. "You did lose, that's true. But I was watching you. I saw you pull back and analyze Justin's weaknesses in less than a minute. You saw that he'd overextend himself when he lunged and that was a perfect time to flip him, and you tried to do it although you didn't know how. You also noticed the way he crossed his legs and left an opportunity to knock him off balance. Again, you went for it. If you knew how to properly pin him, the match would have gone to you. You demonstrated two of the most important things an Elite must be able to do: find their opponent's weakness and go after it with everything they've got."

I gazed at him, struck speechless. That wasn't what I was trying to do. I was just trying to win a silly school match.

But the look in his eyes says this is far from a game.

"As for what we can do for you," he continued, "that depends on what you want. We're all about expanding the Elite Network to include people from all fields and backgrounds. If you get in, you'll be the first member to speak four languages and be so well-traveled. If you lend your talents, we'll lend ours when you need them."

I had no reply. My head was spinning with the implications of what he was telling me. This was bigger than a couple of boys messing around in the woods. The kind of stuff he was talking about made futures and fortunes.

"And then there's you, Grayson." Cameron twisted around to face him. "The only thing I know for sure you want other than pretty girls is to be on top." He threw out his hands. "Well, it doesn't get any higher than the Network, so what's it going to be? Are you in? Are you *all* in?"

Derek scowled. "You say you're on top, but how are we supposed to believe you? Who is in this Network? Name these Olympians and scouts and CEOs."

Cameron didn't skip a beat. "Those are the kind of details you get when you're officially in the Network. You haven't gotten in to the Elite Class. You haven't proven yourself, but... I will tell you this. You already know one person in the Network. He used to change your piss-soaked diapers."

Derek's snarl fled as surprise flashed across his face. "Dad? My dad? But— That's not true!" Derek quickly swung back to anger. "He would have told me!"

"Would he?" He stuck his face in Derek's. "Like I said, you haven't proven yourself."

Derek bared his teeth but said no more. Cameron turned his back on him. "Now, I repeat. Are you in?"

A clear voice broke through the night. "Yes." Landon stepped forward. "I'm in."

"I'm in."

"Me too."

"I'm in."

"Whatever." This came from Derek.

It was down to me and Adam. I was first to move to Landon's side. "I'll do it."

"Okay," Adam spoke up. "Me too."

Cameron's smile sent a shiver skittering up my spine. "Perfect. Now you can come with us."

He and the Elites pivoted and walked off in the direction of the boulder. We were blindfolded when we came in, but they were off now and I didn't need a map to tell me the lights were in the opposite direction. They weren't leading us back to school.

"What is this?" I asked. "Where are we going?"

"You're going to have to trust us if you want to be one of the Elites," he called over his shoulder. "Just remember to keep your mouth shut."

That reply did not fill me with confidence, but the other boys set off to follow them without hesitation.

Adam bumped my shoulder. "Come on. If we're doing this, we're doing it."

I looked between him and the boys disappearing into the trees. "Alright," I said as I let out a shuddering breath. "Let's go."

Chapter Four

The noise pulled us deeper into the woods. I didn't understand the sounds I was hearing. It made no sense. My confusion only deepened when I spotted the glow breaking through the trees. What was going on? Where were they taking us?

Together, we stepped out into a clearing. My jaw dropped.

"Oh no," Adam moaned.

"Dammit, Cameron!" Derek cursed. "You're such an ass!"

The older boy laughed. "Don't be like that. The volunteers always get together during O-Week and throw one of these. You should be happy you're invited, but remember, you keep what we talked about to yourself."

With that, he and his friends walked off and joined the party. Yep, party. Boys and girls were talking, dancing, and drinking if the red Solo cups held what I assumed they did. The rest of the Elite Class was here and some boys from our orientation got the invite, but clearly none of them knew about our meeting by the boulder.

I looked at the kids assembled and then down at myself. Everyone was in their pajamas, but we were the lucky ones without shoes, and in Cole's, Michael's, and Derek's case, they didn't have on shirts either.

"This is not good," Adam whispered.

I glanced up at him, but he was looking in the other direction. I followed his eyes to... Melody.

The girl stood next to the keg holding court. Whatever she was saying must have been interesting because a group of guys and girls were fixed on her as she went on, waving her hands and gesturing.

I elbowed him. "Why don't you run back to the dorm and get changed before she—"

The sentence wasn't out of my mouth before one of the girls she was talking to glanced in our direction. Her eyes bugged at the sight of so many hot, half-naked boys—and me—and she tugged on Melody's arm. Melody turned and looked right at us.

I clicked my tongue. "Too late."

"It's not too late," Adam said. "I'll just go back like you said and—"

I grabbed his arm before he could run away. "She's already seen you. Don't be embarrassed. You've got more clothes on than those guys."

"I'm in my boxers," he hissed.

"So are half the guys here. Own it. Be confident. And use full sentences when you speak to her."

"But—"

I shoved him in her direction and let fate take over. Adam stumbled off as I looked around the party. This was the first party I had been to.

What am I supposed to do with myself?

I wasn't much of a drinker. Mom had no qualms about letting me sip from her glasses of wine or take a swig of her beers growing up, and I accepted fast that I hated the taste. The speakers were pumping a steady beat, but I could not dance for anything. Maybe I was the one who should head back to the dorm. There was nothing for me to do here.

I turned my back on the party. *I'm tired anyway. I'll just—*

"Don't leave so soon." A hand fisted in my pajamas and pulled me up short. "We haven't had a chance to talk."

I didn't get out a word before I was spun around and pulled to someone's side. His velvety silk pajamas caressed my cheek as he pulled me close and enveloped me in his spicy sweet scent. I had a brief thought about pulling away, but it vanished when Landon smiled down on me.

"We all know each other, but you're brand new. If we're about to spend the next four years together, we should lift the veil of unfamiliarity."

We?

I broke away from his gaze as the other boys moved in on us. Cole, Michael, and... Derek.

My heart shot into my throat when I laid eyes on him. "Um... is that your way of saying you want to get to know me?"

Derek scoffed. "I already know you—"

I stiffened. *What? How—*

"—you're another loser fanboy that thinks stalking me online makes you my friend."

I flushed hot. "I'm *not* a fanboy! I just wanted to talk to you."

He raised a brow. "About?"

I swallowed as my eyes flicked between the guys. "It... wasn't important."

"That's what I thought." He looked at the others. "You all waste your time with him. I'm going to party."

Derek strolled off. Within seconds, two girls ran up to him and tucked themselves under his arms.

I shook my head as I watched him go. "What's up with your friend?"

"He's not our friend," Landon replied. "He's not friends with anyone."

"Who cares about him?" Cole stepped forward. "What's up with you? Do you really speak four languages?"

"He does," Landon said before I could reply. "Plus, he's better at math than Santi."

"I answered one question," I cut in.

"Still," Landon went on. "It was enough to impress Cam and that guy does not impress easily."

Cole's gaze turned appreciative. "Nice."

"Why does it matter?" I asked.

"How can you ask that after what just happened?"

Michael closed the distance between us. "We've lived in Evergreen our whole lives," he said. This was the first time I had heard Michael Young speak. His voice was soft and smooth like water passing over a riverbed. It slipped into my ears and stuck in my brain. "We've gone to the same schools and we've known we were headed to Breakbattle since elementary."

"We've also known we were expected to become one of the ten boys in the Elite Class," said Cole. "Just like Moon—even though he likes to play it cool—and Fields. Our parents expect nothing less."

"But we expect even more," Michael continued. "We're going to be better than the best. We want all the privileges that come with being Elite and more." His tone was measured, but his gaze burned into me, rooting me to the spot. "I'm not stopping with Olympic gold medals. I'm going even higher. I plan to break world records."

Cole nodded in agreement.

"That's great," I replied for lack of anything better to say. What did this have to do with me?

Landon gave me a little shake. "Cam was right about my aspirations. I've got plans that Mom and Dad don't know about—that they don't want for me. Which means, I need the right kind of people on my side. We're not friends," he said bluntly as he gestured at Michael and Cole. "But this is bigger than that. We'll be the real players at this school, so we need to know our allies, and it seems... you're going to be one of them."

"So let's talk," Michael finished.

My eyes ping-ponged between them. "Right now?"

"No," Cole said. "Tomorrow. Lunch. Sit with us."

They fell silent, clearly waiting for my response. The expressions on their faces spoke to their seriousness. Why was everyone at this school so intense? I could only imagine what it would be like when we had to battle for everything. Maybe I should remove myself from the craziness now.

"Okay." The word popped out of my mouth. "Tomorrow."

"Good." Landon squeezed my shoulder, and for some reason, my face grew warm. What the heck was wrong with me?

He released me and walked off in one direction while Cole and Michael went another. What was I supposed to do with myself?

I looked around and lit upon a bunch of kids gathered by a blanket. It was loaded down with snacks. If I was staying, I might as well eat.

Pushing through the bodies, I made for the food. I breathed a sigh of relief at the sight of soda and immediately poured myself a cup.

"...can't believe it."

Someone bumped my arm and the soda sloshed onto the blanket. I straightened up as Melody reached for the bottle and tugged it out of my hands. She poured herself a drink while she chattered at the girl next to her.

"I was trying to talk to our team leader about how elitist and discriminatory the class system is and she walked away. What the hell is wrong with everyone? How can they not see how messed up all of this is?"

"You tried to convince one of the Elite that the system is elitist?" I said. "You had to know that wouldn't go well."

"Excuse me?" Melody swung around, her brows snapping together. I braced myself as she looked me up and down. "You know... you might have a point."

I blinked. She was agreeing with me?

I relaxed as I sized her up in turn. She had on a cute pair of purple pajamas with little bunnies on her pants. Her outfit wasn't as sexy as the short shorts, tank tops, and bare chests of the others, but the lift of her chin and confidence in her stance made it clear she knew she didn't have to try. She was already the most beautiful one here.

She's right about that, I thought. *It's no wonder Adam is struck dumb at the sight of her.*

"There's no point trying to convince people who benefit from the system to turn on it, but you'd think they'd feel more solidarity than that." She shook her head. "Well, I'm not going to keep quiet. I'm going to make everyone see we have to get rid of the battle system."

"Good luck. I hope you succeed."

Her eyes narrowed. "Don't patronize me."

"I'm not. Seriously, I hope you do open people's eyes. I've been here a couple of days and I see how harsh the competition can be. Not to mention what I heard about that poor girl, Becca Taylor."

Her expression softened. "Yeah, I heard about her too. They brought her up when they said we'd have to see the therapist twice a semester. It's so sad, but still, it wasn't enough to get them to change."

"It's awful."

Melody didn't reply at first, but I noticed the angry glint in her eye had disappeared. On the contrary, she was smiling.

"What's your name?"

"Zeke Manning."

"Melody Durand." She reached out and shook my hand. "Where are your shoes, Zeke?"

I snorted a laugh. "They're back in my dorm doing me no good." I looked down at the pink, strappy sandals adorning her feet. "But I love your shoes. They look just like a pair I saw in a boutique in Paris."

"Oh my gosh. They are from Paris. From this place near the Eiffel Tower called La Papillion."

"No way! I know it. I went there all the time."

Melody's forehead wrinkled. "You did?"

"For my mom," I said quickly. "I shopped there all the time to get gifts for my mom. She loved that shop."

"Oh. Okay." She ducked her head. "So you like Paris? My family vacations there every spring."

"J'y ai vécu deux ans," I replied. "I lived there for two years."

She giggled—a light and surprisingly sweet sound. "You speak French, and you have good taste?" She released my hand only to place hers on my shoulder. "You're too good to be true."

I beamed. "We'll be on opposite sides of the campus, but it would be cool if we could be friends. We can talk Paris."

The corner of her mouth quirked up into a grin. "Definitely. I'll see you around, Zeke Manning."

I waved her off, smiling away. Most of the people here were strange, but at least I was making friends.

You didn't come here to make friends, a voice reminded me. *There is one thing you need to do and it's more important than anything. Don't get distracted.*

The smile melted off of my face. If I wanted the normal high school experience, I wouldn't be at Breakbattle Academy with a wig on my head. I couldn't lose sight of why I was here. I would make friends when it was all over.

I turned away from the snack blanket...

...and smacked into a hard chest. Soda spilled down my hand as I bounced off Adam.

"What was that? Why were you talking to Melody? You weren't talking about me, were you? Did she say something about me?"

I gaped at him. "Seriously, Moon." I shook the wetness from my hand. "You have to play it way cooler than that."

"You made her laugh." His eyes grew unfocused. "She has the most beautiful laugh, doesn't she?"

Oh yeah. This guy is far gone.

"It's a delight," I deadpanned. "The real question is did *you* talk to *her*?"

He pinked. "I tried, but she was talking to her friends and I didn't want to interrupt."

"Well, try again. This time tell her how great she looks and listen to her plans to bring down the system."

"Good tip but"—his eyes drifted over my head—"I think we need to get out of here."

"What? Why—"

"What on earth is going on here?!"

I swung around and the last of my undrunk soda went flying. A woman in rollers and a thick, plaid robe burst through the trees. It was Vice Principal Argyle. Trailing her with the scruff of his neck firmly in her grip, was one of the boys the Elite had snatched out of bed: Parker.

I had a second for the situation to sink in before Adam seized my arm. "Run!"

That was the cue. Students scattered in every direction, dropping their Solo cups and bolting as fast as their legs could carry them.

"No one move!"

Adam yanked me after him. We escaped through the woods, running and stumbling over tree roots as branches tore at us. We didn't know where anyone else was but we heard them crashing through the woods around us, screaming like getting caught would have more deadly consequences than a talking-to.

Over the thrashing and frantic, panicky cries, there was a strange squeaky sound.

We were laughing. Adam and I were laughing so hard we were tripping over more than the roots. Maybe there was time to make friends.

"I DON'T GET WHY YOU guys were invited and not us," Justin griped. "Cam doesn't even know Zeke."

"Stop whining, man," Zachary replied. "We were at the party for ten whole minutes and then it was busted by Argyle. She's on the warpath now."

On the warpath was right. She didn't manage to catch any of the students after they made a break for it, but she stormed into breakfast that morning and made it clear that if any other kids were caught out of bed after curfew, they would start the new school year with two months of detention.

Her reaction wasn't on the same level as the Elites when she left the room and they turned on Parker. Cameron and Santiago descended on his table, told him to get up, and led him out.

I peered around Adam to where he sat alone on the bleachers. Something about the sight of him head bent and exposed in his swim briefs struck me with sympathy.

I wonder what they said to him.

"Are you really not going to swim? Zeke?"

I started when I realized Zachary was speaking to me. I took my eyes off Parker and glanced down at the massive swimming pool waiting to claim the boys for their next trial. "Yes, I'm not swimming."

His eyes got bigger. "Even after... last night?" he whispered.

"I want to do well on the trials, Zach, but drowning won't get me anywhere. There's nothing I can do."

Owen heaved a sigh. "I can't risk this one either. Mom actually called the school and told them not to let me in the water. I'm going to do the other trials though, no matter what."

The same fervor gripping Owen was humming through the class. Everyone was determined to make up for low scores the day before or maintain their edge. At the top of the bleachers, Cameron and Santiago watched on.

"They're here to see you and Reed," Zach said to Adam, following my eye. "We all know you're both going to top this trial."

Adam didn't appear fazed. He gestured at the entrance as a familiar face walked in. "That's Mom. I'll be right back."

He popped off the bench and took off. Zachary shook his head at his back.

"Hard to figure that guy out sometimes. He acts like he doesn't care, but how could he not? Everyone wants this."

I said nothing. I didn't know Adam that well, but I did know that there were plenty of things to want more. Thankfully, Owen changed the subject and we talked about what we were going to do with the rest of our summers while the clock ticked down to the second trial.

Adam rejoined us just as a man in a tight polo shirt and orange swimming trunks emerged from the locker room. He blew sharply on his whistle, but there was no need. The room fell silent the moment he stepped out.

"Alright, boys. Listen up. My name is Coach Nelson. You can call me Coach." He settled in front of the bleachers and clasped his arms behind his back. "The way we're running this is simple. Five at a time, you will stand up, take your positions, and begin when the buzzer sounds. You will swim as fast as possible to the opposite end of the pool to the touchpad. Your time will be displayed, I will record it, and you will receive your final score based on that. The fastest time will be granted the highest score. Understood?"

"Yes, Coach!"

"Good. Then, there will be no issues and this trial will run smoothly." He pulled out his clipboard. "First five, you're up."

Nelson might have been hoping for smooth, but it was far from that. It turned out it wasn't only me and Owen who didn't belong in the water. One boy jumped in and immediately sank like a stone. The boy could not swim literally to save his life and Nelson was forced to dive in and fish him out. Coach wasn't even mad. He sent him off to get changed and then went back to the trial like nothing happened.

Sadly, it didn't stop there. There were two other boys who could swim, but not well. They flapped and flailed in the water until they finally got to their touchpad long after their opponents. Then there was the guy who couldn't swim straight and veered off into someone else's lane. They collided in a splash that would have been funny if the other hadn't flipped out on the dude for messing up his race. Coach Nelson had to jump in again when they started fighting.

"You still mad your mom made you sit out?" I asked Owen. "Better to fail with dignity than some of these other jokers."

"You may have a point," he mumbled.

Both of us were more than ready to see the final race and the boys that were in it.

"Whooo!" Miss Val bounced on her seat. "Go, Adam!"

He tossed his mom a wave as he stepped up to the platform. On his left was Derek Grayson, and on his right was Cole

Reed. Adam was too focused on his overexcited mom to notice Reed's attention on him, but I saw his look plain and clear. Adam may not have cared about the outcome, but Reed did—big-time.

"Positions, gentlemen!"

Adam turned back to the water and put his goggles in place. He leaned forward and I did too, holding my breath.

The buzzer pierced through the room and Adam flew off the platform in a graceful arc and then disappeared beneath the surface. I could swim, but never in a million years would I be able to cut through the water the way he was. Adam was merely a blur, and on his side, Cole kept pace effortlessly.

Lungs bursting, I half fell out of the seat when their final strokes brought them within smacking distance of the touchpad. They stuck their heads out of the water and whipped around to the scoreboard where everyone was looking, uncaring of the other boys still swimming their race.

The air whooshed out of me in a torrent of disbelief when the times flashed across the boards.

"I can't believe it," I whispered.

Adam and Cole had tied—right down to the last millisecond.

"Fuck!" Cole punched the touchpad, earning a sharp whistle from Coach.

Adam's reaction was simply to heave himself out of the water and stride off.

Day two of the trials was complete.

"YOU WERE INCREDIBLE," I gushed. "For real. I didn't know humans were capable of swimming that fast. You were nothing but a streak. I think I even saw Coach Nelson smile."

Adam laughed from beneath the cloth. He was sitting at his desk with nothing on but a pair of shorts and a towel over his wet locks. After the trial, we went back up to the dorm to chill before lunch.

"Thanks, Zeke."

"But Cole looked like he wanted to burn the place down."

"Cole doesn't like to lose, and yes, he sees a tie as losing."

I shook my head. "I forget you all know each other. So none of you are friends?"

"Michael and Cole are cool, but nah, we haven't been friends since elementary school."

"What happened?"

He shrugged. "It's just not as simple as when we were kids."

I let it drop. I knew by now they had a history. If Adam wanted to tell me, he'd do it in his own time.

I heaved myself off the bed. "I'm going down to lunch. You coming?"

"Nope. Mom wants to take me out to celebrate. I'll catch up with you later."

I shoved my shoes on and headed out. The cafeteria was near empty when I stepped inside. No girls to take up half the seats so I had my pick. I took my fish tacos to the table at the back and got comfortable. Three trays smacked down next to me seconds after I brought one to my lips.

"Where's Moon?" Cole asked by way of greeting.

I blinked at him, Landon, and Michael. "He's having lunch with his mom."

"Good."

Landon's hand passed in front of my face. "You going to eat that?"

"I—"

He snagged my apple off my plate. My eyes followed the theft until they connected with his now pink orbs. The contacts had been changed up.

"I was going to eat that," I finally said.

Landon cocked his head. "Yeah? You can have this instead." He reached for my hand at the same time he pulled something out of his pocket. His palm was warm on my skin as he nudged my fingers open and heat surged through my body.

The reaction confused and annoyed me at the same time. *The guy just touched you. Stop acting like the weirdo everyone thinks you are.*

Landon placed something on my palm before releasing my hand. "People think I like apple-flavored things so they're always giving me this stuff."

I put the apple candy chews on my plate and then tucked my hand in my lap. It was tingling strangely.

Landon reclined back in his seat, eyeing me as he munched on the stolen apple. He looked amazing, as usual. Cole's hair was still wet from his shower, but Landon snuck in time to wash, dry, and style his raven locks. It matched the expensively casual air he was going for with the button-up shirt, bow tie, and suspenders.

Cole and Michael should have been eclipsed by him, but not even jeans and plain shirts could diminish the pull of Michael's almond eyes or the cute way Cole wrinkled his nose as he plucked the tomatoes off his tacos.

"So what's your story, Manning?"

Landon's question ripped me back to reality. "What? Oh. There's not much to tell." I pointed my eyes down to my food. "It's like I said on the first day. I've lived in a lot of places and—"

"Forget that," Cole broke in. "We're not talking about the past. Tell us what you want. Why are you at Breakbattle?"

My grip tightened imperceptibly on my fork. "Lots of reasons."

"What do you want to do?"

"I don't know," I admitted. "Something with math. I love it."

"That works." I glanced up at Michael's voice. "Math's not our area. Cole and I are going all the way. Him with swimming and me with track and field."

I eyed Landon. "What about you? Do you really not want your parents' companies? Because you wear them well."

He chuckled. "Henrietta and Declan insist I represent the family brands at all times. I bought a pair of jeans once and they vanished from my closet the very next day." He shrugged lightly. "But it's fine. I have other plans and they have nothing to do with math. So none of us are your competition on that front."

"I never thought you were my competition."

"You should," said Cole. "Everyone here is your competition, homeschooler."

"That's not going to become my nickname, is it?" I asked lightly. I picked up my food and took a bite.

"It won't if you stop acting like one. This isn't your momma's living room. We're going to be the next Elite Class, and we'll only be as strong as our weakest classmate. You need to see everyone as competition because that is how they see you."

I gave him a salute. "Gotcha."

Landon let out a gusty sigh. "Forgive him. He doesn't know how to turn it down."

That comment earned Landon a glare hot enough to set his bow tie ablaze. Adam was right about one thing. These guys weren't friends.

"Aren't we supposed to be getting to know each other?" I cut in, drawing Cole's attention away. "You're so worried about me being the weakest link. What about you? What are your best subjects?"

"Physics," said Landon.

"History," Michael replied.

"Chemistry," Cole said.

The three responded as quickly as you do when someone asks your name.

"Moon has English," Landon continued. "Derek's got biology and Fields can do whatever the hell he does. With you on math, we're set next year."

Cole waved a hand. "Hold up. We don't know if this guy is really as good as people are saying. We're supposed to spend our afternoons studying for the placement test. We'll study together and see what you know."

I looked at them in surprise. "We are? We will?"

"Yes."

"But Argyle didn't say we had to study."

Cole pinned me with a look. "Nope, and that's why all the future F Class kids will be sitting on their ass all afternoon. Not us."

"You seriously want to study together? You guys don't seem to like each other or me."

"Being friends isn't a requirement for becoming Elite. We just have to know that when people come for us to battle, you'll be able to defend what's ours."

Goodness. This guy really doesn't know how to turn it down, but it's not like it would hurt me to study.

"Okay. Fine."

"We'll go up to my room after we're finished."

With that settled, the guys polished off their food and pushed back from the table. They looked down at me expectantly as I shoved the last of my taco in my mouth. Under different circumstances, I would have liked three hot guys eager to get me alone for a study date, but in this getup, not so much.

You like it just fine, a traitorous voice spoke up, *or your heart wouldn't be banging like a drum and your palms wouldn't be getting sweaty just thinking of Landon touching you. You've never had a crush before, but it seems that's changed.*

I shoved the thought down as I rose from my seat. The boys led the way out of the cafeteria.

"Hey, guys, wait!" Zachary skidded to a stop in front of us. "Where are you going?"

"We're going to study."

"I'll come with."

"Who said you were invited?" Cole snapped.

Zachary's smile faltered. "Come on. I'll be one of the Elite too. We'll be hanging out and studying all the time. Might as well get used to it."

Cole grunted and stepped around him. Zach seemed to take that as a yes, because his smile returned. He rushed off after Cole while the other guys followed, but I didn't move. I looked back toward Owen and Justin's table. Zachary had run off so fast he hadn't even taken his tray.

"Manning, what's the holdup?"

Michael stood in the entrance, waiting for me. I tossed one last wave at Owen and Justin before picking up my feet and following him.

"You know," I said as we passed by the smiling faces of alumni. "There are more important things than being in the Elite Class, and if you think I'm a crush-everyone-on-the-way-to-the-top kind of person, then let me wake you up from that dream right now."

"I agree."

"And another thing, I—" I halted as what he said penetrated. "Wait. What did you say?"

"There are more important things than the Elite Class," he repeated, "and those things are the opportunities that come from being in it. You know about my mom."

"No."

He squinted down at me, frowning, but after a second his face cleared. "Sorry. Homeschooler. I forgot." He took a deep breath, and for a moment, the blank, serious mask that had been his face lifted. "My mom is Elaine Young. She was a champion and headed straight for the Olympics. Track and field. It wasn't a question. That was until some stupid drunk ran through a red light and put her in a wheelchair."

"Oh no," I breathed. "Michael, I'm so sorry."

He looked away. "It was years ago. The point is, I'm doing this for her. One day, a Young is going to bring home the gold and that's going to be me. I didn't know about the Elite Network before last night, but now that I do, I have to get in."

Of all the stuff I had heard from Cameron, Santiago, Cole, Adam, and the rest, this was the first time I really understood what being in the Elite Class could mean.

"I get it. I know you'll get there. You'll bring back the gold."

Michael met my eyes... and smiled—a full, real, beautiful smile that punched me in the gut.

Cheeks warming, I tore my eyes away. *Make that a crush times two.*

"Thanks, Zeke."

I mumbled something in response.

Our group reached the dorms and climbed the stairs to the fifth floor. We passed my room and kept going to the final door at the end of the hall.

"I brought my textbooks," Cole said as he unlocked the door. "You guys can go and get yours. We'll meet back here in ten minutes."

Michael, Zach, and Landon split off. Cole frowned at me when I didn't move.

"I didn't bring textbooks."

He rolled his eyes like he expected nothing less from me and then shoved into the room. I followed after him, hiding a smile. I wasn't trying to rile him up, but it was kind of funny how intense he was.

I walked inside and our eyes met instantly. My grin froze on my face.

Derek shot up in bed. "What the hell is the stalker doing here, Cole?!"

"I'm not a—!"

"Chill, Derek," Cole said mildly. He strolled over to his desk and gathered his books. "We're going to study for the placement test. You can join us if you feel like taking a break from being an asshole."

"Fuck you."

Cole flipped him off over his shoulder.

I watched the exchange with wide eyes. I wasn't sure if Cole had a talent for pissing people off or if Derek was just the kind of guy who hated everyone. Either way, I was glad they were focusing their ire on each other.

"Sit down, Manning," Cole said without turning around. "There's an extra notebook on the couch. You can use that."

Derek watched me through eyes narrowed into slits as I crossed the room. I felt the weight of his annoyance like an anchor on my chest. I sat in the chair with its back to him just to get away from his stare.

Cole was still fiddling around his desk. For lack of anything better to do, I took out my phone and messed with it while I waited. Minutes passed, but no words did. The room was completely silent.

I quickly got bored of my game and clicked to my home screen. *I should text Adam and tell him—*

"That your girlfriend?"

I yelped as I flew off the couch and my phone went flying. Derek was leaning over the cushions. A smile played on his jerk face. He was obviously pleased with himself for scaring me.

I snatched my phone off the rug. "What do you think you're doing?"

He shrugged. "Had to make sure you weren't sneaking pics of me and posting them on your creepy perv site."

"Wonderful," I said, blank-faced. "Now I've gone from a stalker to a pervert with a website. Are you like this with everyone who makes the mistake of sitting next to you?"

"Nope. Only the special few." Derek flipped over the couch and landed with his legs crossed and arms folded behind his head.

I bet he's practiced that move.

"So that girl on your screen," he said. "Is she your girl-friend?"

I looked down at the picture of me and Jordan cheesing at the camera. We had taken it the first time I transformed into Zeke. "No, she's my cousin."

"Nice. She's wicked hot. Let me have her number."

"Negative."

His grin only got wider. "She won't thank you for that. I'm Derek Grayson. Most girls would kill for my number."

"You're not her type. She doesn't date pricks."

"Who said anything about dating?"

"Okay. We're done talking about Jordan." I grabbed his legs and swung them onto the floor. "You were super busy brooding in a corner when I came in. I don't want to keep you from that any longer."

He stood up without a fight. "Alright, perv, but if I see you point that phone in my direction, I'm breaking it."

I barely contained an eyeroll as he wandered back to his bed. He stretched out on the sheets and picked up a book from the nightstand. The scowl lines left his face, and for a minute, I saw the guy from the cafeteria who laughed with his whole body. Derek almost looked... sweet.

Knock. Knock.

Cole opened the door for the other boys to come in.

"Are you kidding me?!" Derek raged. "Why are all these people in my room?!"

I sighed. So much for sweet.

I stayed out of it while Derek went back and forth with the boys. I was already the creepy stalker perv. I didn't need to collect any more nicknames.

"Cam thinks we're going to be Elite," Cole argued. "If we'll be in the same class, we need to get a feel for what everyone knows and where we have weaknesses."

"Oh, *Cam thinks*," he mocked. "What the hell does he know? None of us have taken the test, and stalker freak here has already flunked the swimming trial."

Great. I'm a freak now too.

"Cam doesn't know any more than you do what class you're going to be in, so stop swallowing that bastard's bullshit."

I had heard nothing but harsh words from Derek since I met him, but this was different. This time there was real venom. He did not like Cameron Dupre.

"Maybe not," Cole replied. "But I do know that this is my room too and we're not going anywhere. So join us or shut up."

Growling, Derek flipped over and gave us his back. I could practically see the anger radiating off of him.

Cole stomped over to the table and slammed his books down. "Math first," he snapped. "I heard the math test starts at ninth-grade level and then gets harder until you can't do anymore. Let's see how far Manning can go."

I sat crossed-legged on the carpet and grabbed the notebook. "I'm ready."

"Me too." Landon surprised me by opening up his own notebook and taking a seat next to me. I tensed when his knee brushed mine. "I'm good at math too since physics is my game. If you can keep up with me, you're definitely good."

"Let's do it."

Cole cracked open his math textbook and flipped until he found a question. "Okay. First problem: what is negative five over six times negative six over seven?"

My hand flew across the page, but not even it could keep up with my brain. I relaxed as the numbers zipped across my mind.

Everything in my life was uncertain. If I was honest, my life has been uncertain since I was an infant setting off for the first time to a new world. Homes, friends, faces, foods, and cultures could all change in a blink, but math never did. No matter where I was in the world. The rules of math were always the same. Two plus two was always four, and the answer to this question would always be—

"Five over seven."

Cole pulled a face. "That was an easy one." He took another minute to search out a problem. "Write this down: If Martha took a trip to Washington that took five days..."

I copied the question, mind whirling as I calculated in time.

"I got this one," Landon stated. "Okay, if it took five days, then—"

"Martha left on the twelfth."

Gaping at me, Landon dropped his pencil. "How do you do that so fast?"

Zachary elbowed Cole. "Stop giving him easy ones."

"Yeah. Try this." Michael took Cole's textbook and replaced it with his phone. "This is twelfth-grade algebra."

"Okay." Cole had a glint in his eye like he finally had me. "Find all sides of a right triangle that…"

I wrote down the problem and then paused. The clock ticked while Landon scribbled furiously next to me.

"Look at that," Cole goaded. "We stumped you. I guess Cam was wrong… about…."

He trailed off when my hand shot across the paper. I broke down the equations, plugged it into the theorem, and finally solved for x and y. I couldn't stop the smile that came to my lips when I wrote the final number. This was fun.

I held up the notebook with the answers displayed and all four guys stared at me.

"Alright." Cole shoved the textbooks to the floor. "It's on now."

Half an hour later, I was the only one on the floor. Zachary, Michael, Cole, and Landon ended up on the other side of the table as the math battle the likes of which Breakbattle had never seen raged.

Landon leaped on the couch. "I've got it! He'll never get this one! What is six hundred and fifty-two times eight thousand and twelve?"

"Starting the clock," Michael said as I quickly flipped to a new page. "One minute!"

"One?" I cried. "I had two minutes on the last one."

"Are you admitting defeat?!" Landon demanded.

"Never!"

I wrote faster than I ever had in my life. The numbers peeled themselves off the pages and danced in the air until they came together to form the answer.

"It's five million—"

A chorus of groans cut me off before I could finish. I rocked back, howling as I fell onto the carpet. I don't know when exactly this turned from a test to a game, but somewhere along the way we stop competing and started having fun.

Landon lost his stuffy bow tie when he flung it across the room. Michael fell off the chair twice, laughing. And I hadn't seen Cole scowl for a full twenty minutes.

I rolled over, clutching my sides, and my eyes lit upon Derek. He was looking at us and... he was grinning.

"That's it," Zachary shouted. "I'm ending this right now! Manning, what is fifteen times eleventy bajillion?"

I screwed up my face. "What?"

"You have one minute."

"Michael!" I protested. "This is what it's come to? You can't win fair and square?"

Landon leveled a finger at me. "You started it. You didn't tell us you were a freaking human calculator."

"Thirty seconds!"

"Fifty times eleventy bajillion, Manning," Zachary carried on. "Or the Evergreen boys take it!"

I couldn't help it. I cracked up at the extreme ridiculousness of the entire situation. These guys were nuts, but for the first time, I was looking forward to being in the Elite Class. "Okay," I shouted between guffaws. "I admit defeat!"

No sooner had the words left my mouth than they cheered.

Amid the chaos, I looked over at Derek. Our eyes met and, for a moment, he smiled with me. A feeling I couldn't comprehend took over my body. It filled me with a lightness that threatened to buoy me up and float me to the ceiling. I had no trouble believing he had dealt with his fair share of obsessive fans. One look at that smile and it sucked you in.

A million thoughts and feelings flooded me as Derek Grayson and I looked at each other.

Until he blinked.

His face smoothed out, and then he ducked his head and went back to his book.

Chapter Five

Adam laughed as he handed me a tray. "So I go to one lunch with my mom and you become friends with Landon, Michael, and Cole?"

"I don't know. I trounced them in a math quiz and then they resorted to frankly pathetic tactics to win. Does that make us friends?"

"Sounds like it to me."

"Then, yes. That's what happens when you go out to lunch."

We busted up as we piled breakfast onto our plates. The truth was I was practically skipping over yesterday. It had been a long time since I had that much fun goofing off with people my age. I wanted this. I wanted to get into the Elite Class. I wanted to push my math as far as it could go. I wanted to be the team the boys thought we would be.

And it wasn't just because my heart thumped whenever Landon put his arm around my shoulder or Michael smiled at me or Cole made that cute annoyed face. That was just a bonus.

"What about Derek?" Adam asked while we headed for a free table. "Was he cool?"

My smile dried up like a dewdrop in the desert. "Let's see. When I packed up to leave, the guy accused me of holding back Jordan's number because I wanted her for myself. So I've graduated from a creepy stalker pervert freak to trying to get with my own cousin. What is up with him?"

"Why did you want to sit with him? Do you know him?"

"Never met him before the other day." I ripped open my milk carton and took a swig. "I only wanted to talk to him. I thought we could be friends. He seemed so nice when I first saw him."

"Don't take it personally. He's like that with almost everyone. Eventually, he'll get tired of hating you and move on to someone else."

I took a bite of my cereal rather than reply. What Derek said had stung. I thought for the barest moment that things were okay between us and then he brought that hope crashing down. I didn't know where to begin with that guy, but I wanted more than for him to go from hating me to ignoring me. If we were going to be in the same class, I wanted us to be friends.

A hand rested on my shoulder, tugging me from my musings. "Hey, Zeke."

I twisted my neck and looked up into Melody's smile. "Hey."

A choked noise sounded from the other side of the table.

Melody took no notice. "That was so crazy the other night, right? I can't believe that Parker guy went to Argyle."

"It was so crazy. We were just saying how crazy it was, right, Adam?"

"Um... yes."

"Cool," Melody replied. "Anyway, Matron went ballistic. She's been patrolling the halls at night and waking everyone up with her hacking cough."

"Matron?"

"Yep. Just another way life is unfair on the girls' side. Matron is in charge of our dorm. I'm guessing they trust you guys to look after yourselves."

"We don't have a matron or anyone like that. That's unfair, isn't it, Adam?" I looked at him with huge eyes, sending him telepathic waves to say something.

"It's unfair," he repeated.

"Tell me about it." She sighed. "Anyway, I've got to go. My friends and I are warming up for the racing trial. Good luck."

"Thanks."

Melody turned and walked off, but not before tossing one last smile over her shoulder. "You too, Adam."

The minute she was gone, he pounced on me. "What was that?"

"Me? I was going to ask you that. Why didn't you talk to her? She was standing right there."

"She was there talking to you," he replied. "Are you guys friends?"

I shrugged. "Yeah. I guess we are."

He threw up his hands. "I've been trying to get her to notice me since preschool and you become her friend after a couple of days." He carded his hand through his curls, somehow not messing them up. "I know it's my fault, but my brain turns to mush whenever she's around."

I know the feeling, I thought as I spotted Landon walking into the cafeteria. I didn't have an apple for him today, and my silly heart twinged with regret. If this is what crushes were like, I certainly understood Adam better.

"Give it time. She'll get to know you and see how amazing you are."

Adam laughed. "Alright, Mom."

I winced. It was harder to control these slipups than I thought it would be. Time to change the subject.

"Are you ready for the running trials?" I asked. "Michael said yesterday that he was going out early to warm up. Maybe we should too."

"Early for Michael is four a.m."

"That's because he's a true champion." We hadn't noticed Cameron sliding up to our table. His shadow, Santiago, was right behind him. "Everyone expects him to win today and he's not going to let us down."

I noticed that wasn't a question.

"Did you need something, Cameron?" Adam asked.

"Yes." He held out his hands. "Your phones. We're giving you our numbers."

Adam and I shared a look. I couldn't think of a reason not to hand over the phone. Actually, it would make it easier to pelt him with the questions I still had.

I passed it over. The boys typed their numbers in, handed it back, and moved on to Landon's table.

"Do you think the administration knows?" I asked Adam though my eyes remained fixed on them. "About the Elite Network? Or their recruiting tactics during orientations?"

"No, they don't."

"How can you be sure?"

"My mom is friends with Argyle. She would have told my mom something like that and then Mom would have told me. More than that, she wouldn't have enrolled me in this school."

"But how can they operate under everyone's noses like that?"

"By making sure people are too afraid to talk. It's worked before."

I shifted around and faced him. "Why did you say yes to Cameron that night? Are you hoping that the Network will get you to where you want to be?"

"No. I know that I don't need them to get far in life. Either way, I'm taking over for my dad and bringing the company to new heights. The only question is if getting there will be easy or difficult, and saying no to Cameron Dupre is the quickest way to make it difficult."

I swung my head back to the handsome, smiling boy. There was nothing in that perfect face that said he would make trouble for anyone, but I trusted what Adam and my own sense told me. I was more than happy to keep him smiling. Making an enemy of Cameron was not what I came here to do.

The two of us finished our breakfast and went up to our room to change. I was doing this trial and even though I didn't expect to place anywhere near the top, at least I could get points on my score.

Owen and Justin caught up to us when we stepped onto the lawn. Together the four of us headed out to the track where most of the boys were already huddled in front of the bleachers.

"Ready, Owen?" Justin asked. "Time for you to come back hard after yesterday."

"I'm ready. This is the one trial I should be able to do without a problem. There's no way I'll be able to get into A Class, but at least I can become a C."

Adam squeezed his shoulder. "Where you're placed isn't where you have to stay. You'll only be a C for a semester. Then you're with us."

Owen beamed, standing a little taller. "Thanks, man."

I smiled. *Adam is amazing. Melody will see that.*

"Are you sure you're going to be okay?" I piped up. "Don't push yourself too hard. Your arm needs to heal properly."

Owen laughed. "You sound like my mom. I'll be fine, Zeke."

I cleared my throat. "Right, yeah, of course. Tough it out."

If I keep this up, Mom will be my nickname, not Homeschooler.

"Boys, your attention, please!"

The call brought our chatter to a dead halt. Together, we formed a group around a slim man with a cap and whistle. The cap was pulled low on his forehead, casting shadows on his eyes, but his smile I could see without a problem. It was wide, beaming, and showed off all of his teeth. The guy was brimming with excitement for the trial to come.

But he doesn't have to do the running, I thought while he rattled out instructions. *But at least he seems nice. All of the other coaches so far have been so serious.*

"—is Coach Potts," he announced. "Today is simple. You'll race in groups of five. The winner of each group will move on to the next race. The others are done for the day. This will continue until the last five students have raced and we've determined the number one in the class. Understood?"

My eyes drifted off Potts and sought Michael in the crowd. I finally found him in the back next to Cole. My heart thumped at the sight of him.

His running clothes hung loose, but still his shorts and tank did nothing to hide his sculpted body. Every inch of him was lean, hard muscle and it tantalized like the look on his face as he laughed with Cole. Beams of light fell across him and made his copper skin gleam as he tossed his head back.

Wow. He is so—

Michael lifted his head and our eyes met.

I jerked. *Oh my gosh. He caught me looking. What do I do? What— He's coming over here!*

"Alright, everyone," Coach Potts sounded. "First five, take your places. The rest of you grab some bleachers."

My class set off in the opposite direction while Michael kept coming toward me. I stiffened with every step.

He's coming. What do I do?

Just play it cool, my internal voice said. *Stop acting like a lovesick teenage girl. He's not that hot.*

Michael jerked his thumb over his shoulder. "Zeke, come sit with us."

"Okay." I practically tripped running after him. Who was I kidding? The guy was so hot that looking at him too long would burn out your retinas.

Michael and I sat down next to Cole on the bottom seat, giving us the perfect view of the race. We watched as the five students took their positions. Some looked confident. The others looked like they wanted to lie down and give up right there.

Coach had just sounded his whistle when a slight nudge on my arm made me look away.

"When you go, remember to breathe properly," said Michael. He spoke to me but kept his eyes on the race. "No quick, shallow breaths. You have to breathe steady and deep. Also, keep your head straight and don't hunch your shoulders. You need to maintain the right form."

I pulled a face. "Are you giving me tips?"

"Obviously," he said with a chuckle.

"Why?"

"You said your homeschooling mostly consisted of sitting at the table with a math book glued to your hand. Breakbattle might not think so, but I don't think it's fair that you have to compete against all of us when you haven't done much running." He nudged me again. "Besides, if we're really going to be Elite, we have to help each other."

"Is that a good idea?" A smile played at my lips. "Aren't you afraid I'll blow past you in this trial?"

He grinned back at me. "Not even a little. I'm winning this one, Zeke. Everyone knows it."

I might have teased him about being arrogant if it wasn't for the matter-of-fact way he said that. It didn't sound like bragging. Michael spoke like one who simply knew that they were the best and pretending otherwise was a waste of time.

"Okay," I said instead. "Then, I'll take all the tips you've got. I read last night that you shouldn't clench your hands, but you also shouldn't let them flop. So what are you supposed to do?"

"Right. You want to hold your hands like this and..."

Michael and I chatted through most of the trial. It was halfway in that I felt something on my neck and turned around to find Owen practically on top of me, listening in. He wasn't the only one.

Michael looked amused at the sight of them. "You guys have questions too? I'll answer them."

The tide was unleashed.

"Michael, how do I run faster?"

"Michael, what's the right way to strike the ground?"

"Michael, how do I improve my breathing?"

In ten seconds flat, I was shoved down the bench and five guys were between me and Michael.

I stood to get away from the shoving when Coach called, "Next group! Manning, you're up."

Four other guys got up from their seats and joined me on the track. None of them were in my orientation group, so I didn't know how good they were or how screwed I was. I wasn't moving on to the next round without beating them and I needed big points to make up for sitting out the swimming trials.

Just focus on what Michael said. Face forward, hands relaxed, shoulders back, and breathe. I can do this. I repeated the mantra to myself as my heart slowed. *I can do this.*

"On your marks!" Coach bellowed. "Set!"

"*Eeeek!*"

I took off. The track lay before me, stretching into a sea of reddish-orange and white lines. Beside me, my opponents huffed and puffed. Their arms swung wildly like they were hoping to sprout wings and soar to the finish line.

"Face forward, Zeke. Don't look anywhere but ahead."

I heeded Michael's voice. Turning away from the others, my world narrowed until I could see nothing but what existed between my white lines.

In. Out. In. Out.

My breathing centered me as I curved around the first bend. I wasn't choking or gasping to fill burning lungs like the other rare times that I ran. I felt fine. No, I felt good.

I put on a burst of speed, just to see if I could go faster, and my legs responded to the challenge.

Beads of sweat collected on my forehead, but I couldn't risk the distraction of brushing it away. My heart pounded in time to my feet and my body felt perfectly in sync for the first time in my life. So this was why people ran.

I curved around the final bend and—

"*Eeek!*" Coach blew sharply on his whistle, startling me to a stumbling halt. "Winner! Zeke Manning."

What? I won?

I whipped around and saw the others trailing me, still running around the final curve. I had done it. I won.

Cheers went up in the stands. Adam, Owen, Justin, and Michael were on their feet, whooping. I zeroed in on Michael, and before I knew it, I was off the track and throwing myself at him.

"Nice job, Ze—" I grabbed him and squeezed hard enough to hear a grunt. "Okay. We're hugging now."

"That was amazing!" I gushed. "I did everything you said and it worked. I can't believe it!"

Michael laughed, although he didn't hug me back. "Course it worked, but you're not so bad. A natural."

"I loved that," I said as I released him. "It was like being in my own zone. I never got why people woke up every day to run around in a circle, but I totally understand it now."

"Don't get too excited." A drawl to my left drew my attention. Cole gave me his patented scowl. "You haven't advanced to the final race yet."

He had a point, but I wasn't letting him pop my bubble. Everyone here had a top subject and a top sport. Even if I never got on Michael's level, running could still be mine.

"Next group," Coach called. "And you, Manning. Hit the water station."

Michael and I went in opposite directions. I headed over to the cooler while he stepped up to the line. I stood there sipping the chilled water as Coach put the whistle to his lips.

He blew and I almost choked on the drink. Michael shot off in a torrent of gasps from the stands. My eyes widened as I watched him pull so far ahead, I knew there was no chance his challengers would catch up to him. At that moment, I knew what everyone else did: Michael Young was winning this trial.

"MICHAEL WAS AMAZING. Coach actually pulled him aside after and said he expects to see him on the team in the fall. None of the other coaches said anything like that."

Adam pulled ahead and pushed open the door to the dorms. He held it for me. "They're not supposed to. We can't get any clue to how we did on the trials until after the scores go up, but everyone knows Michael plans to follow in his mother's footsteps. Coach Potts isn't missing his chance to train a future Olympian."

"It's like a whole other world over here," I said as we climbed the stairs. "I've lived in places where all that needs to be achieved is feeding your family, building your home, or finishing your education, but here people are working to take over companies, represent their country, or be known as the best in the world. Everywhere you go, we're all the same, but still so different."

Adam didn't reply right away. I glanced over at him and spotted his amused smile.

"Sorry," I said. "My cousin said I like to get poetic. It's just that being here makes me wonder what I want out of my future.

There's so much I can do with math, but I haven't sat down and thought about what."

"You might have a career as a runner if the math doesn't work out. You made it all the way to the final fifteen. Not bad."

It wasn't so bad considering I came in third behind the guy who won that race. Coach even thumped my back and sent me off to the showers with a smile. I didn't leave even though all the other students who completed the trial left at the first opportunity. I hung back and watched the final race between Adam, Michael, Cole, Derek, and a kid named Lars Johansson. Michael finished long before them, but the other boys' times were impressive.

"Tomorrow is basketball," I said as we entered our room. "Are you secretly brilliant at that too?"

Adam laughed. "No way." He stepped up to his bed and reached for the hem of his jersey. I immediately turned my back when he peeled it over his head. "I played with my dad once when I was six. He tossed it at me, I missed, and it hit me in the face. I ran crying to Mom and never played again."

I burst into giggles at the mental image. "Not even in your gym classes?"

"Got out of it by practicing with the swim team. Things don't fly at you in the pool. I'm all for that." I heard movement behind me. "I'm going to hit the shower unless you want to go first?"

"No, you go ahead."

I waited until the door closed before sitting at my desk. I had gotten an idea while I was talking with Michael, and now, I finally had a chance to check it out.

I pulled a notebook out of my desk and then sat down at my computer. When Adam came out of the shower, there were three notebooks in front of me and twelve tabs open.

"What's all this?" I sensed a presence over me and my nose was filled with the scent of pine and sandalwood. "Are you studying for the placement test?"

"No, I'm studying for tomorrow."

"Tomorrow? How can you study to play basketball?"

"Adam, it's so cool." I swung around in my seat and found myself inches from his bare chest. I quickly swung back, cheeks hot. I didn't like Adam like that. What was the point when he was smitten with Melody? But it was still strange for me to be around guys with their shirts off. I had lived in a lot of places, but Mom had kept me pretty sheltered.

I need to talk to him about getting dressed in the bathroom.

"What's cool?"

I cleared my throat, focusing on my notes. "Michael was giving me tips before the race, and while he was talking, I thought this was just like math. You have rules. There is a right and a wrong way to run, just like there's a right and wrong way to solve a problem." My voice got higher with excitement. "So what if instead of thinking of sports as something you can or can't do, you think of them as math problems."

"Uhh. You lost me."

"Look, look, look." I got up and shoved Adam into my seat. I pointed to the screen. "I found a bunch of websites that say the same thing. People don't think about it, but there is math in basketball too. Dribbling and making shots is all about geometry. You need to understand arcs, distance, and height."

Adam took a minute to scan the website and look over my notes. "This is pretty smart," he finally said, "but I don't think that's all there is to it, or every math whiz would dominate the court."

"Trust me. Math is in everything, and once you understand it, the rest falls into place." I patted his shoulder. "This will work."

IT DIDN'T WORK.

I huffed down the court, trailing my team as they chased after Derek like lost ducklings who spotted their momma. I don't know how good the guy was at math, but he was incredible at this.

I watched through my sweaty bangs as he jumped, toes hovering inches from the ground, and tossed the ball over grasping fingers. It dropped through the basket with a swish that couldn't be heard over his whoop.

Zachary from my team snatched up the ball and ran it back to our side. I hurried to keep up. Skirting the other guys, I skidded to a stop on the edge of the court while my team surrounded Derek and the other side went for Zach.

Over their heads, Zach locked eyes with me.

No. Oh no—

"Manning!" Time slowed as Zachary tossed me the ball. Out of instinct, I lifted my arms above my head and it smacked into my palms. As soon as I brought it down to my chest, all eyes turned to me. Maybe it was a mix of exhaustion and dehydration, but I swear those eyes were glowing like beings from below.

Swiftly, I spun toward the basket and lined up my shot.

You can do this, Zela. One minute to go and no one in front of you. You're four inches over five and six feet from the goal. If I hit the exact angle with the correct force, I'll make it.

Heart rocketing in my chest, I moved my hands down a fraction and then tossed the ball. It sailed from my hands in a graceful arc, destined for only one place. The smile stretched across my face as—

Something flashed across my vision and smacked the ball out of its path. "Whoo! Not in my house, cousin-lover!" Derek dove for it when it bounced back and snatched it up before I had a chance to blink. He tore down the court and all I could do was watch with my mouth hanging open as he made the final shot to the raucous sound of the buzzer.

It was over. Derek's team won.

I trudged off the court, picked up my towel, and headed straight for the door. There was no reason to stick around since that was the final game of the day.

The wind streamed over me as I stepped outside. Summer was bringing its dreaded heat, but the breeze cooled the sweat on my skin. All I wanted was to crawl in the shower and wash the game from my body.

"Hey, Zeke. Wait up."

I slowed down as Adam jogged over to my side. "There may be something in your basketball math thing. You were good."

"What are you talking about? We lost."

I had managed to make three shots, but halfway through the game, I lost my breath and never got it back. Michael's breathing tips didn't help as much when you're zipping and zagging all over the place and catching elbows in your gut. I struggled to stay on top of Derek and my dribble game was nonexistent. One thing math did help me with was calculating the seventeen points we lost by.

He shrugged. "Your team was bound to lose with Jose, Justin, Parker, and Derek on the other side. Especially Derek. The guy could be his own team."

"That's right, Moon."

I whipped around. Neither of us had noticed Derek come up behind us. Sweat had darkened his dirty-blond locks until they appeared almost black. Despite this, he wasn't winded or falling over like I was about to. That gorgeous smile hung on his lips, telling of how much fun he found the trial.

"I'm going to be captain of the team before the end of our first year so Cameron better look out." He tossed an imaginary ball into an imaginary hoop. "Coach Singh was watching me like I was the answer to his dreams. I'll be captain and"—he pinned me with a look—"there won't be any cousin-lovers on my team."

I frowned. "What are you talking about? Who said I wanted to join the team? And I'm not trying to get with my cousin!"

He ignored my outburst. "You can shoot. That much is obvious, but you're too slow. You stand there for a century staring at the basket before you take the shot."

My brows shot up my head. How had he noticed all of that while running around the court?

"I have to," I protested. "I'm..."

"You're what?"

"I'm doing the math."

"What the hell does that mean?"

I looked away. "It doesn't matter." The last thing I needed to do was give Derek Grayson more reason to make fun of me.

"Whatever. One more day of these stupid trials and then we can get this placement test over with." He backed away, tossing over his shoulder, "See you after dinner, Moon."

"See ya."

I looked between Adam and Derek's retreating back. "What's happening after dinner?"

"We're going to study," he replied as we set off for our dorm again. "I'm going to test him and he's going to help me with bio. Derek likes to pretend he doesn't care, but his dad would lose his mind if he didn't get into the Elite Class."

"He would?"

"Oh yeah, but don't tell anyone we're studying. He swore me to secrecy."

A niggle of hope unfurled in my chest. "Can I join you guys? The three of us can study in our room."

Adam threw me an apologetic look that said it all.

"Never mind." I sighed. "Derek won't study with me."

"No, but he was right about you being a decent shot. If that really was because of your math stuff, you should see if you can apply it to soccer."

I perked up a little. "Hmm. That's not a bad idea."

We went up to our room, showered, and chilled until dinner. Adam went down to the cafeteria with promises to bring me something to eat while I remained glued to my computer. Researching soccer math had taken me down the rabbit hole of sports math in general. I wasn't sure if any of it could really help me, but it was fascinating.

I was halfway through my third stashed granola bar when my phone rang. I glanced at the screen before hitting accept.

"Hey, JoJo. What's up?"

"Good. You're using your girl voice, so you're alone." A clang sounded over the speaker. "We're about to have dinner. Mom is making your favorite."

"Briyani chicken with mushroom pakoras?"

"Your other favorite."

"Ah. Baked spaghetti."

"She'll make it again when we pick you up on Monday. So how's it going? Has anyone found you out?"

"Amazingly, no." Memories of being pulled from my bed and dragged through the night pierced me. "But something strange did happen. It's too weird to tell you over the phone. We'll talk about it on Monday."

"Okay. What about your roommate? Is that weird too?"

"He's actually really nice. Adam has been telling me everything I need to survive this place."

"And"—Jordan lowered her voice—"what about the other thing? Did you—?"

"What are you whispering about over there?" Auntie's voice was faint but couldn't be missed. "What is Zee getting up to?"

"Tell her I'm being the perfect gentleman."

"She said she's— Wait. Mom!"

There was a scuffle and then Auntie came on the line. "How are you, Zee? Ready to come home yet?"

"Not yet." I pushed my laptop away and leaned back onto the pillows. "Everything is fine, Auntie. I promise. I can handle myself."

"I know you can, but it's not too late to enroll you on the other side."

"But it is. The trials are almost over."

"No, I've spoken to your vice principal and as long as you take the placement test, students can still start in the fall. You'll just have to take zeros on the rest you missed."

I stiffened. "You spoke to the vice principal about me?"

"Relax. I told her I was asking for Jordan—no one else. The point is you can end this without a problem."

"No problem except for zeros on my trials and everyone wondering what I was trying to pull by pretending to be a boy. The few friends I have would drop me."

"Zee—"

"Auntie, please. I know what I'm doing. Trust me."

"I would if you weren't lying to me. I know you're not doing this for any book. You might have spent most of your life far from me, but I know you, little niece. Something else is going on here and whatever it is, you can talk to me."

This wasn't her stern disapproval or her amused sarcasm. Her concern was reaching through the phone and burrowing inside of me.

"I just want you to be happy and safe, Zee. You've been through so much."

"I know," I croaked. Tears stung my eyes and I roughly wiped them away. "But you have to believe me. I need to be here."

I listened as she took a deep breath and held it. After a few seconds, she slowly let it out. "Okay. I'll let this go... for now."

Those final words didn't fill me with too much reassurance, but I'd take what I could get.

Jordan came back on the line. "Hey, you okay?"

"I'm fine."

"So, what about...?" Jordan trailed off, but I didn't need any more details.

"Nothing to report. It's only been a few days though."

"Call me if you need me, okay?"

"I will."

We said goodbye. I tossed my phone on my bed and reached for my laptop again.

"Wait..."

My head snapped up.

"Please, wait!"

The computer almost fell to the floor as I whipped around, but nothing met my eyes but an empty room.

"Wait!"

"No." I scrambled back and tipped over. Crashing to the floor, a sharp pain shot through my elbow, but I kept crawling until running into the dresser stopped me. "No, no, no, no. Not again. Not again!"

"Wait for me..."

I clapped my hands over my ears, but that couldn't drown out my sobs. Memories I thought I buried long ago rose from the depths and dragged me under.

Chapter Six

A chorus of screams, shouts, and piercing whistles echoed across the field as the players ran around like ants. It was the final day—the final trial—and a fervor gripped the boys. This was their last chance to impress the coaches and then it was all down to the placement test. They were feeling the pressure while I was feeling nothing.

The players were blurs in my vision as I gazed at the soccer field through unfocused eyes. *Why did it happen again? I thought it was over. I came here to end it.*

"Zeke?"

The voices have to stop. They should have stopped. I'm better now. I—

"Hey, Zeke."

A nudge jerked me out of my thoughts. I shifted around and Adam came into focus.

"Are you okay? You seem out of it."

I nodded.

"Are you sure? You've been quiet all morning and you didn't eat breakfast." His concern was etched into his face. "Stressing about the trial?"

"Yeah," I replied when I found my voice. I pushed my fears down and locked them away. I wouldn't deal with this. I couldn't. "I stayed up late researching soccer math, but I don't know if it will help."

"It can't hurt. Besides, I don't think you have to worry so much about this crowd. Coach Fineman looks like he wants to fling his whistle and run out of here."

"What?" I looked down the stands at Coach. The bridge of his nose was pinched between two tight fingers. I hadn't paid a lick of attention to the game, but I focused on them now.

It was a disaster.

Most of the boys clearly didn't know what to do besides kick the ball, but some couldn't do even that right. Justin reared back, angling for the goal, and whacked the ball with all his strength. The heads of those in the stands followed it as the ball went whizzing our way and narrowly missed taking out Coach.

Red faced, he scrambled to grab his whistle and jammed it in his mouth. Sense returned before he blew and he yanked it out and threw it down. He wasn't allowed to say or do anything unless the boys did something dangerous. He was forced to sit out this mess with the rest of us.

"Oh my goodness." Justin and Landon dove for the ball at the same time and collided with a smack that made me wince. "What is happening out there?"

"It's not surprising. Most of us graduated from Evergreen or Chesterfield Middle and neither school teaches soccer. The only guys who learned how to play did from their families or outside teams and, as you can see, not even they can save this game." Adam clapped a hand on my back. "For the first time this week, we're on equal footing."

"Why does that make me feel better?"

We laughed and the last traces of my misery fled. Everything was going to be okay. I knew what I needed to do. I just had to focus on why I was here.

Adam's gaze flicked over my shoulder. "Incoming."

I turned around just as Cameron and Santi stepped up to our row. The boys walked up to us, but made no move to sit.

"Yes?" I squinted at Cam through the glare of the sun. Once again, I was struck by the charm of his smile, but this close, I could see it didn't reach his eyes.

"There's a party tonight to celebrate the end of the trials." He gestured at Santi. "Our group plus Dominic and Tyler's group, and a few of the girls are coming. Last chance to have some fun since everyone will be pulling an all-nighter tomorrow to get ready for the placement test."

"Is that a good idea?" I asked. "What if Argyle catches us?"

"Yeah, Cam," Adam piped up. "It's not worth the risk. I'm going to stay in and study tonight."

Cameron's smile didn't falter. "I'm sorry. Did it sound like I was asking? Let me try again: There is a party tonight and you both will be there."

"Why?" I asked.

"You didn't think becoming one of us was as easy as a chat in the woods? The placement test isn't the only one you need to pass. We'll see you tonight."

With that, they turned and left. A thread of unease nagged at me as I watched them go.

"A test? What kind of test?"

"One we won't like."

If I was worried before, my anxiety ratcheted up to a thousand at Adam's reply. Was this some kind of hazing? What would they do to us if we go?

What will they do if we don't? I can't face being yanked out of bed and dragged through the dark again.

"Next match!" Coach Fineman called. He waved the others off. "You guys hit the showers."

The players trudged off the field—a ragtag bunch of sweaty messes covered in grass, dirt, and a few bruises. Our match did not go much better.

I tried using soccer math to make goals but only managed one. Having to stand still and make calculations wasn't suited for a fast-moving game like soccer. The ball was kicked out from under my feet half a dozen times, and off again I went chasing after it.

The game ended two to zero in favor of my team. I was praying that getting one of those points meant I did well on this trial, but who knows. What I really cared about was dragging myself to my bathtub and sinking my tired muscles into water that was near boiling. I'd never worked, ran, or exercised as hard as I had that week.

"The results of the trials will be posted on Monday," Fineman told us as we gathered our things to go. "Good luck to all of you."

I waved goodbye and then hurried to catch up with Adam. We headed up to our room, washed off, and then pulled out our things to study. We worked in silence—Adam at his desk and me on my bed with my laptop—as the clock ticked down and the light retreated through the windows.

Our phones buzzed around eight o'clock. Adam put down his pen and read the group text. "Cam says the party starts at eleven and we're supposed to meet him behind the basketball gym."

"Are you going?"

"He doesn't give us much of a choice."

I sighed. "That's true."

We fell silent as we went back to our work. I wasn't sure how to study for the test or what to focus on, but I had notes saved on my computer from years of homeschooling, so that seemed a good place to start.

As it got closer to eleven, I noticed the both of us were spending more time looking at the clock than we were paying attention to our work. At ten forty-five, I called it quits.

"Let's just go."

Adam didn't argue. We got up, shoved our shoes on, and headed out of the door. Adam spoke up when we were almost to the first floor. "We don't look like we're about to go to a party."

"More like we're visiting the undertaker."

We laughed a little at that, but quickly sobered. I wasn't crazy about risking two months detention on some "test," but they gave me a chance to back out and I refused. I wouldn't be chased away from the Elite Network. I just hoped I could handle whatever was coming next.

Adam and I made it outside without issue. No one passed us in the halls. No vice principals chased us in hair curlers. We skirted around to the back of the gym and discovered we weren't early. Landon, Cole, Michael, Zachary, Cameron, and Santiago were all here.

"Waiting on Grayson," Cameron said, "and then we'll go."

"Are you going to tell us what this test is?" Cole asked.

"When you're all here."

His tone invited no argument, so I leaned against the wall and settled in to wait. I figured that wouldn't be long, but eleven came and went with no sign of Derek.

Cameron glanced at his watch. "Where is he? He's ten minutes late."

"I'll text him." Santi pulled out his phone and the glowing screen lit up his face as he typed.

A faint chime sounded moments after he put it away.

Derek rounded the corner as we all turned our heads. "Was that you messaging me?"

"What took you so long?" Cameron demanded. "We told you eleven o'clock."

He made a face. "Shut the hell up, Dupre. I'm here, aren't I? Let's get this over with." Derek stormed off, striding toward the trees without a glance back. After a pause, we followed him.

Twigs snapped beneath our feet and critters scurried through the night, but our group remained quiet. Soon Derek fell back and let Cameron lead us farther and farther away from the school.

Just how far are we going? I get not wanting to get caught, but we could get lost going this deep. Who would want to party so far out here?

A chilling thought went through my mind. *What if there is no party?*

I stopped cold, dread filling my bones. What the heck were we walking into?

"Zeke?" Adam stopped and peered back at me. "What's wrong?"

I raised my voice. "Why are we here, Cameron? What is this test?"

"Yeah." To my surprise, Cole stopped walking too. "Tell us what we're supposed to do."

"We're almost there," said Cameron. "Just hurry up."

"No," snapped Derek. "Tell us now."

"I said hurry up!"

Cameron must have been annoyed because that was the first time I heard him yell. He didn't slow down and we were forced to keep going or get left behind.

Several minutes passed before I heard the rhythmic bumping of music. A few more minutes and I heard the talking and laughter to go with it. We passed through the copse and finally stepped out into a clearing. The party wasn't as packed as the first one, but there were still plenty of students dancing, drinking, and making out against the trees.

"Alright." Cameron stopped on the fringes of the party and gestured for us to get closer. "This is how it's going to work." His brown eyes swept over us, meeting our gaze in turn. "The most important skill you need to survive is how to find your opponent's weaknesses and use them to your advantage. Sometimes it's as easy as paying attention like Manning does, but most often it's not that simple—"

"What's the point of this?" Derek growled. "Just tell us what we're here for!"

Cameron's eyes narrowed. His calm and collected mask was cracking. "I'm getting to that, Grayson. Like I was saying, some secrets are buried too deep and you need to find a way to dig them up."

"Secrets?" I asked.

"That's right. Your task for tonight is to get someone here to tell you something they've never told anyone. One of those deep, dark secrets they prayed would never get out."

I gaped at him. "How are we supposed to do that?"

The other guys shared my look of disbelief.

"Figuring that out is the whole point of the test."

"This is stupid," Derek stated. "I'm not doing it."

Cameron's lips curled. "Why am I not surprised you'd be the first one to quit? You were never cut out for the Elite Network."

"I'm not quitting the Network! I'm just refusing to do this shit!"

Cameron's eyes flashed. "Everyone who is invited in must do it. If you refuse, you can't join us."

"Bull." Derek elbowed me to the side as he advanced on the older boy. "I bet you made up all this kidnapping and tests crap because you have nothing better to do with your life."

"Guys, come on." Adam stepped in the middle of them. "Cool it."

"I don't need to do this anyway," Derek plowed on. "If my dad is in the Network, then I'm in too."

"You think so?" Over Adam's shoulder, I saw Cameron smirk. "Then, why didn't he tell you about any of this before? If you ask me, he knew you'd screw up, so why waste air telling you about it. Face it, Grayson. You're a fucking disappointment and everyone—including your dad—knows it."

"What did you say?!" Derek launched himself at Cameron—shouting and swearing. Adam, Landon, and Michael rushed to hold him back.

I cast a look over my shoulder and saw half the party was staring at us.

"You're wasting time," Cameron said over Derek's noise. He didn't sound bothered by the fact that Derek was trying to rip his head off. "You have two hours to bring me a secret or you're out. Get going."

Derek shoved out of Adam's hold and stomped away, disappearing back into the trees. I looked around at the other guys. Part of me wanted to go after him, but he made his feelings for me very clear. I doubt my presence would help him, but the alternative was going into that party and...

How could I do this? I thought as I turned toward the chilled-out crowd. Even if I could get someone to spill their secrets in two hours, turning around and sharing it with everyone was just slimy. What would Cameron do with information like that?

He told us what he would do. Exploit their weaknesses.

A hard pit lodged in my stomach, but I forced myself to join the party. This was worse than hazing. They weren't trying to hurt me. They were forcing me to hurt someone else.

I scanned the faces. We weren't the only people I recognized. Justin and Owen were standing by the drinks, talking to a couple of girls. A few feet from them wearing a simple, sleeveless dress was Melody.

I made a beeline for her. "Hey, Melody." She turned at my voice. "I see you got past Matron."

She laughed. "Luckily there is only one of her. We snuck out while she was on the top floors. I see you've got shoes on this time."

"I like to mix it up."

Melody's giggles were probably helped along by the drink in her hand. I spotted her flushed cheeks and bright eyes. She was well on her way to getting drunk. No wonder Cameron made us do this at a party.

"How did the rest of the trials go?" I asked.

"It was good, but I'm glad they're over." She sighed. "Not that I want to take the placement test either. I just want to get out of this place and go back to enjoying my summer."

"What's summer like in Evergreen?"

"Oh, it's perfect," she replied, beaming. "My parents and I travel for part of the summer, but when we're home, I go to the beach every weekend, eat ice cream at the Promenade, shop with my friends. What do you do?"

"I'm usually in a different place every summer, but now that I'm back, my cousin wants to take me to—"

A hand gripped my forearm and pulled me back. "Can you excuse us for a second, Melody? I need to talk to Zeke."

She shrugged. "Sure."

I tripped after him as Adam hauled me off. "Hey," I cried. "What are you doing?"

"What are *you* doing?!" he hissed. "If you think I'm going to let you manipulate her for Cameron's stupid little game—"

"Adam, come on." I ripped my arm out of his grasp and planted my hands on my hips. "I would *never* do that. I'm sticking close to her so that no one else comes along and tries to take advantage, you dolt!"

He blinked at me. "You were? Oh." He had the decency to look sheepish. "Sorry."

"You should be. I want to get into the Network, but not like this. I'm not participating in this test."

Nodding, he looked over at Melody. "You're a good guy, Zeke. I forgot that for a second. Thanks for looking out for her."

"She's my friend too." I shoved his arm. "But why don't you take over? Go talk to her about summers in Evergreen."

"I... think I will." He backed away. "Thanks, man."

I waved him off, shaking my head. I watched as within minutes they were deep in conversation. Adam finally spoke to her and it only took the threat of Cameron and the Elites hanging over our heads.

Without them to talk to, I wandered around the party and chatted with random people. At least it would look like I was playing along.

"I learned how to make it while I was in Korea," I said. "Bulgogi is one of my favorites."

"My mom owns a restaurant," said Kim. This was the first time we had talked even though I'd seen him in the cafeteria a few times. "She taught me how to make all kinds of stuff. I wish cooking had been one of the trials. I would have killed that."

"I wonder why they choose those five sports."

"I think it's because—"

"Hey, Manning." I peered over my shoulder and found Cole behind me. "It's time."

My good mood evaporated. "Right. I'm coming."

I said bye to Kim and followed Cole out of the party. The other guys were waiting for us—even Derek. Without a word, we left everyone behind and once more trailed Cameron and Santi through the dark. It wasn't until I spotted the boulder through the trees that I recognized where we were.

We stepped into the clearing, but it wasn't empty. The other Elites who took us that night were waiting for us. Cameron took his perch on the rock and made us line up in front of him. "Alright. Let's hear it. What did you find out?"

No one spoke.

Cameron pointed at one of the boys. "Cole. Speak."

"Fine." He stepped forward. The line of his shoulders was as taut as a bowstring. "I was talking to..."

I hummed loudly in my head. Sang, thought of old movies, recited things I needed to know for the practice test. Anything to distract myself. I did not want to hear this stuff. None of this was right.

"Manning!"

I jerked. "What?" Was it my turn already?

"What's wrong with you?" asked Santiago. "Pay attention."

I pressed my lips together rather than say anything, but Santiago kept his eyes on me while Cameron called the next name.

"Adam, share your secret."

Adam stepped forward. I hadn't been watching him. I didn't know if he ended up speaking to someone other than Melody.

He'd never take advantage of a drunk Melody, but please tell me he didn't find someone else.

A cold sweat broke out on my skin as though it wasn't my own secret he was about to spill. I was quickly starting to see

Adam as one of my best friends and now I had to watch him do something awful.

Adam cleared his throat. "I have a secret."

"We're listening."

He lifted his chin high and looked Cameron right in the eyes. "Something that no one knows... is that I'm in love with Melody Durand."

Wait. What?

Cameron's smile slipped. "Excuse me?"

"You heard me. That's my big secret. I love Melody."

"You do?" Zachary asked, sounding genuinely surprised.

Whispers broke out from the others. They were looking around like they had no clue what to say or do while I just stood there. What was Adam doing? Had his feelings for Melody truly been a secret?

Frowning, Cameron pushed himself up and jumped down. "What the hell are you playing at, Moon? Your task was to—"

"To share a secret from someone at that party. I was at the party and this is my secret that no one knows."

"Really? No one knew before tonight?" His voice rose. "You expect me to believe you haven't been telling your boys all about your little Melody wet dreams. Fields!"

The boy jumped.

"Did you know?"

Zachary tossed his head. "I had no idea, Cam. I swear."

Cameron turned on me. "What about you?"

"I didn't know," I said without hesitation. "So there, Cam. Adam followed your rules. He passed."

"Zeke's right." I swung my head around at Michael's voice. "You didn't say it couldn't be our own secret."

Cameron's lips peeled back from his teeth until his snarl distorted his handsome features. "You think you're pretty smart, Moon?" He stalked toward him, getting right in Adam's face. "But that's the stupidest fucking thing I've ever seen. What kind of idiot exposes his own weakness? I was right about you. You're soft." His hand flashed out and shoved him. "You're too soft to be in the Network, and too soft to take over your daddy's company." He shoved him again. "You'll always be soft!"

Adam straightened and calmly brushed off his shirt. He met Cameron's glittering eyes steadily. "You say I don't have what it takes, but it seems to me beating a bully at their own game is way more impressive than getting a drunk teenager to spill their guts. I passed, Cameron. Say it."

I wasn't in the middle of their staredown, but yet my heart was beating like a drum.

"Alright, Moon," said Cameron. He slowly fixed his jacket and smoothed back his hair. The cool and collected Cameron was reappearing before my eyes. "You passed."

Adam turned and walked back to the line.

"But don't think you won't regret this."

If Adam was worried about that final parting shot, his face gave no indication. He took his place next to Zachary without a word.

"Zach, you're next," said Cameron. "And if you pull the same shit as Moon, you're out."

"No, no," he said quickly. Zachary stepped out into the middle of the circle. "I have a secret."

"About who?"

"It's about... Owen Price."

I blinked. *Owen? That couldn't be right.*

"Zach?" Adam frowned at his back. "What are you doing?"

"Be quiet," Cameron snapped. "We're listening, Fields."

"It's that— It's—" He took a deep breath. "Owen used to fantasize about our middle school English teacher... Mr. Eckheart."

"Zach!" Adam cried.

Zachary pushed on, forcing the rest out in a rush. "He thinks he might be gay, but he's not sure."

"What the hell, Zach?!" Adam bellowed. "What is wrong with you?! He's your best friend!"

Zach flinched like the words were a physical blow but said nothing. He shuffled back to my side while I gazed at him through wide eyes.

"Alright, Manning. You're up."

I didn't speak right away. I couldn't take my eyes off of Zachary although he refused to look back at me. How could he do something like this to his own friend?

"What's your secret?" Cameron pressed. "Or did you not get one?"

"Oh..." I said softly. "I've got a secret. Although I think by now everyone knows." I raised my voice and let it echo through the clearing. "Zachary Fields is so desperate to be accepted that he'd ditch and betray his best friend since preschool."

Zachary's head snapped up.

"It's not even about getting into the Network. He just wants the attention and popularity that comes with being on top, but what he doesn't know is that he'll never get the adoration he really wants because everyone sees him for the sneaky, pathetic person he is."

Zachary flushed beet red. "Hey! Back the fuck off! I just did the test same as everyone else!"

"You're a—!"

I halted. A noise was filling the space—one I hadn't been expecting. Cameron was... laughing?

Cameron cracked up so hard tears streamed down his face. I backed away, not knowing what to make of his reaction. Eventually, he got control of himself. "I said you were observant, Manning. You've got Fields pegged. I'd think we'd all agree by now that wanting to be popular is his weakness."

If it was possible, Zachary got even redder.

"You pass, Manning."

I didn't respond. I wasn't trying to pass this test or get his approval and it didn't make me feel any better to have it. I didn't know Owen that well, but he had been nothing but nice to me. I knew why I needed into the Network, but this isn't who I am. Zeke was only ever supposed to be a costume. I'm still Zela.

"Alright, let's wrap this up." Cameron turned on the final boy. "Derek, what did you find out?"

"You want a secret? I've got one for you."

My brows furrowed. Something in his voice made me look at him. *Why is he smiling?*

"Well, I don't know if you can actually call this a secret since most people suspect but can't prove it." He strode out in front and turned his back to Cameron. It was to us he spoke. "There's been a lot of talk about Dupre Financial Holdings and just how much of that money is dirty."

All traces of mirth vanished from Cameron's face. "Grayson—"

"But the answer is," Derek continued, "all of it! His dad is up to his filthy, rotten neck in gang money, stolen pensions, bribes, and all sorts of things the SEC frowns on." Derek even scrunched up his face in a little pout. He was enjoying this.

"Grayson!"

"He's got money sacked away in so many extradition countries that he's got Manning beat, and despite Cameron's act—strutting around like he's above everyone else. The truth is he's nothing but the illegitimate son of a worthless crimin—"

"Argh!" Cameron launched himself at Derek.

I let out a scream as they fell to the ground in a tangle of limbs.

"Motherfucker!" Cameron grabbed him and flipped him on his back. Spittle flew from his mouth as he raged. "None of that is true! Take it back!" He lifted a fist clenched so tightly, his knuckles turned white. "I said take it back!"

Derek laughed in his face. "Make me."

Santi grabbed his arm before Cameron got his chance. Shouting, he was hauled off Derek by his friend and two of the other sophomores.

Derek was still laughing as he got to his feet. "Trying to beat me up? I expect nothing less from the son of a thief."

Cameron let out a roar. His hand shot through the shield of his friends, clawing at Derek as he fought to escape their hold. "I'll kill you for this, Grayson! Do you hear me?! You're going to be fucking sorry!"

"Wow, you're mad." He carelessly brushed off his clothes. "What was the point of this game? Finding your opponent's weakness and using it against them. Well, I've done that, so this means I pass." His voice turned hard. "I guess I'm not a disappointment to my dad after all."

Cameron screamed such horrible things at him it made my stomach churn. I don't think I've ever seen naked hatred before. It twisted his face beyond recognition.

"That's enough!" Santi yelled. "All of you, get out of here. Now!"

Derek didn't need to be told twice. He sauntered off without a word, looking nothing but pleased with himself. After a minute, I followed and Adam fell in behind me.

We didn't speak. We didn't look back. But Cameron's words stayed in my mind long after his shouts faded.

Chapter Seven

Saturday brought a new day, but not new worries. Adam and I stayed at our desks, studying for the placement test, but thoughts of the night before were so loud I could hear them coming from both of us. In the end, neither one of us had done something to be ashamed of, but still, a strange feeling hung over me.

I didn't know what was going to happen now. My phone didn't buzz with a message from Cameron or Santiago and I wouldn't step out of the room for fear of running into the others. We survived on snacks we brought from home and tried to focus on our last task.

It wasn't until we woke up on Sunday morning that I broached the topic. "Hey, Adam?"

"Yeah?" He smacked the alarm clock off and heaved himself out of bed. "What's up?"

"That stuff with Melody... are you going to be okay?"

"I'll be fine." He reached into his wardrobe and started pulling clothes out. "Once I made up my mind to give up one of my secrets, I had my pick of which ones to share. Loving Melody isn't something to be embarrassed or ashamed about. I've done worse."

"I can't think of you doing anything wrong. You're a good person—much better than Cameron and it's not because of who his father might be. He never should have asked us to do that." I shook my head. "I wish I believed it would end here, but I have a feeling that with the Elite Network, this is just the beginning."

Those words hung in the air between us as we dressed and got ready for breakfast. We would eat first and then the placement test began at nine o'clock on the dot in the multipurpose room. Big enough to hold us all while the faculty stood watch.

The cafeteria was packed when we stepped inside, but this time there was no shouting, laughter, or banter back and forth. Students sat huddled up at their tables with a fork in one hand and a textbook in the other.

Adam and I loaded our trays with pancakes and hash browns and then took them to a table in the back. "You think we're ready for the test?"

"As ready as we'll ever be," Adam replied. "I just want to get it over with."

"Me too," I said. "Let's talk about something else. What are you going to do when you go home?"

"We're going to the water park. What about you?"

"My mom will be working on her book, but my cousin is going to introduce me to her friends. We're going to spend the rest of the summer being normal teenagers before Breakbattle claims me."

He chuckled. "There won't be anything normal about our lives then."

"Tell me about it." I cut a slice of pancake and popped it into my mouth. The doughy, syrupy goodness was helping to lift my mood. "I still wonder how they came up with all of this. Why they chose those five sports and the system they use to determine placement and the winner of battles. I've been looking it up, but when they're quoted, the staff just give standard answers."

Shaking his head, Adam gave me a strange smile.

"What? What did I say?"

"I see why you're so good at math. You never stop until you find the answer."

"I think that's a compliment."

"Don't worry. It is."

We laughed, enjoying a light moment, until I spotted something over Adam's shoulder.

Santiago came into the cafeteria and marched directly up to Landon's table. My grip tightened on my fork while I watched them talk. I couldn't look at him without picturing him holding Cameron back as he fought to make good on his many terrible threats.

Santi straightened and looked right at me. He headed for us while Landon stood up and went over to Cole and Michael's table. "You need to come with me."

"Why?" Adam asked.

"Now. It's important." Santiago didn't look bored or annoyed at that moment. He just looked serious. "Get up."

He moved off toward Zachary's table, clearly expecting us to follow.

Adam and I shared a look. "What do we do?"

"We won't hear the end of it if we don't go," he said. "Let's just find out what he wants so we can finish our food."

We pushed back from the table and made for the doors. Cole, Landon, Michael, Zachary, and Santiago met us just outside the cafeteria.

Santiago didn't stop. "Let's go."

"Wait," I called. "Derek's not here."

"Come on!"

Not knowing what else to do, we followed him through the halls and out onto the quad. The other boys tried asking him questions, but Santiago refused to speak. He stared straight ahead as he led us past the gyms and in the direction of the woods.

"Seriously?" Adam piped when we realized where we were going. "We don't have time for another 'club meeting.' The test is in less than an hour."

Santiago did not acknowledge that he heard him. There was a tense silence hanging over the boys while we headed deeper. As though everyone was recalling what we went through the last time we were here.

What if this is about the other night? He could be dragging us out here so they can tell us Derek is out of the Network.

I gazed at the back of Santiago's head. It's not like he would tell me, so I just have to wait and find out.

The older boy took us down a path that was becoming familiar to me. When we stepped over a gnarled root, I knew we were close to the boulder.

Santiago was first to enter the clearing and I heard a voice.

"There you are. Are they here?"

"They're all here."

Adam pulled out ahead of me. "What is going on?" He burst through the trees. "Why did you—" Adam stopped so abruptly I ran into his back. "Oh no, Cameron... what did you do?"

"What?" I moved around him. "What's wrong..."

I trailed off as I took in the scene. It was as though a bucket of ice water had been tipped over my head. I stood frozen. My legs couldn't move to run. My lips too numb to release my scream.

Cameron staggered toward us. He wasn't the perfectly put-together picture of beauty and charm any more. His hair hung in messy, sweaty lanks. The sleeve of his shirt dangled off of his wrist and a streak of dirt was being washed from his face by tears. But it wasn't him I was staring at.

It was Derek Grayson, lying still at the foot of the boulder. His expression so serene he could have been sleeping if not for the dark, growing pool beneath his head.

"No," I whispered. It was all I could get out before air deserted me.

"Fuck, Cameron!" Cole shrieked. "What did you do?!"

"It was an accident! I swear!" Cameron ran at him, but Cole reeled back, tripping over his feet. Cameron turned on the others, eyes huge and pleading, but they all backed away from him. Except me. I couldn't move, couldn't breathe, couldn't think for the roaring in my ears.

"I brought him out here t-to talk to him." Cameron's voice reached me from far away. "To get him to take back the stuff he said about my father. It was him who took the first swing! I pushed him off and— and— he fell." A keening wail tried to pierce my fog. "It wasn't my fault! It was self-defense. He just fell and hit his head."

"Why did you bring us here?!" Michael cried.

"Because he's— he's dead."

That one word struck me with the force of a blow and something shattered. "Derek," I rasped. Before I knew what was happening, I was running. "Derek! Derek, no!"

I threw myself down next to him. Seizing his body, I pulled him to me. "Don't be dead. Please, d-don't be dead." Sobs ripped from my chest, forced through a throat so tight I choked on them, but I couldn't stop. "Der—"

Rough hands grabbed me and hauled me off.

"No, stop!"

I fought viciously in Santiago's hold, but his arms were steel bands. He crushed me to his chest. "Stop it! Calm down!"

"Calm down?" Landon repeated. "How are we supposed to calm down? Cameron killed Derek!"

"I didn't kill him! It was an accident."

Adam's face was starkly pale. "We need to call the police." He scrambled for his phone. "Or an ambulance. Maybe it's not too late. He could be—"

"No!" In a blink, Cameron launched himself at Adam and wrestled the phone away.

"What are you doing?!"

"You can't call anyone. You weren't here, okay. None of us were here."

"What does that mean?" Landon looked hard at Cameron. "Tell us why you brought us here. Now."

"People... saw us at the party." Cameron glanced back at us and Derek's body. "They saw me and him get into it and then you guys watched him provoke me afterward. You heard the things I said. If they question the students, it's all going to lead back to me, but I didn't mean for any of this to happen. The police might not believe it was self-defense if you tell them I threatened him. That's why you can't say anything."

I stopped struggling, stunned. *What was he saying?*

"Not only that, but you have to say that I was with you before breakfast and we were— were studying or something. Alright?" Cameron whipped around, gazing wide-eyed into each shocked face. "Alright?!"

"I can't—" Cole inched back. "I can't do this."

"You have to! We're brothers now, Cole. You have my back, and I promise, I'll have yours. Whatever you need. Whatever you want!"

"You swear it was self-defense?" All eyes flew to Zachary. He broke his silence for the first time since walking into the clearing.

Cameron nodded frantically. "I swear. He came at me. He started the fight."

"Then... okay."

"Okay?!" Adam shouted. "What's okay?!"

"We all know how Derek is." Zach stepped out of the trees. "You saw how he was the other night. He pushes people's buttons for fun. He loves pissing everyone off and he's been nothing but an asshole since middle school. I believe he started the fight, and if he did... there's no reason Cam should get in trouble for defending himself."

"No," Michael cut in. "We're not doing this. Call the police, tell them the truth, and it will be fine."

"You can't call the police!" Cameron shouted. "You're in the Network. We have to stick together."

"We didn't sign up for this," Cole shot back. "Not murder!"

"I didn't kill him!" Cameron's chest heaved with rapid pants. The wild fear hadn't left his eyes, but I could see something else creeping in. "Fine. If you won't say I was with you... then I'll say you were with me."

"What are you talking about?" asked Adam.

"I'll tell the police we were all here, a fight broke out, and Derek died. People have seen us together. Parker and Jose know you've been recruited. I'll say a hazing went horribly wrong and we were all responsible."

My hair stood on end as he spoke.

"They might believe you if you say I'm making it up," Cameron continued. "Or they'll think you're trying to save your own skin. You won't have to risk it if you agree to say we were together studying."

Landon stared at him, mouth hanging open. "You wouldn't."

"Don't make me."

No one spoke, but as the boys turned to each other, I could see the looks on their faces. I saw them giving in.

"No!" I reared back and dug my elbow in Santi's gut. He let out a sharp grunt and his hold loosened. Falling to the ground, I scrambled away. "I won't let you get away with this! You killed him and I'm telling the police the truth!"

I leveled a shaky finger at him. "It was you who started all of this! You provoked him! You forced us to do that sick test and then you attacked and threatened him when it was turned on you! Accident or not, I won't help you hide from what you've done!"

I yanked my phone from my pocket.

"No!" Cameron surged forward, bursting into a run. "Give me the phone!"

9-1—

Cameron seized my wrist in a grip that made me cry out. "Let me go!"

"Help me!" He fought to wrestle the phone from my grip. "Hold him down!"

Zachary rushed to his side. I opened my mouth to tell him off when he reared back. Zach's fist connected and snapped my head around. Pain exploded in my jaw and I dropped like a stone, releasing my grip.

"Hey!"

Black spots danced in my vision as my head struck the ground.

"You take care of him, Moon," Cameron said. "We have to get out of here. Remember, we were all together."

I heard the sound of retreating footsteps as two hands took me under the arms and lifted me up. The last thing I saw before Adam threw me over his shoulder were the boys slipping through the trees, leaving us alone with Derek's body.

"YOU C-CAN'T DO THIS."

Adam carried me through the woods. My tears dripped down my nose and stained his back.

"This isn't you, Adam. We have to call the police. We have to tell them the truth."

"Of course we're telling the truth."

"We—" The plea lodged in my throat. "What?"

"We're going to get help. Cameron took my phone too, but we'll find my mom and she'll take care of everything. She'd never believe any story Cameron or the others made up about me. We'll do the right thing by Derek."

My tears slowed to a stop. "But— but— Why didn't you say anything back there?"

"They were scared, desperate, and not thinking straight—especially Cameron. There was no reasoning with them. I let them go so they wouldn't try to stop us. By the way, are you okay? Zach hit you pretty hard."

"I'm okay," I said softly. I don't know why it continued to surprise me how good of a person Adam was, but it had been the worst morning imaginable. I couldn't believe anything that was happening. "You can put me down."

Adam stopped and set me on my feet. For a second, we just looked at each other. "Thank you," I whispered.

"I'm sorry. I can see his death affected you."

I turned away. "We should go. We have to find your mom."

Adam led the way, quickening his pace when we spotted the school through the trees. "She'll be in her office. Come on."

We raced across the quad and ran into the school. We passed a group of boys as we darted through the hall and one broke off. "Hey, Adam? Zeke?" called Justin. "Where are you going? The multipurpose room is this way."

"We'll catch up," Adam said.

Together we hurried past the cafeteria and turned into the faculty hallway. Adam burst into a run at the sight of his mom's door. He tugged on the handle, but it didn't budge.

"She's not here."

I bounced on my heels. "Where could she be? Are you sure she's at work?"

"She's here. She must be in the bathroom or in the faculty dining room."

"Then, you check the dining room, and I'll look in the bathroom."

"Wait, Zeke—"

I took off down the hall. I wouldn't wait. I needed to find her.

I rounded the corner and threw open the door to the bathroom. I may have been dressed like a boy, but I was still a girl and this was an emergency. "Miss Val? Miss Val, are you here?"

No one answered my call. I ducked out and ran back to her office in time to see Adam appear at the end of the hall.

"She's not in the dining room," he said as he jogged over to me. "She's here some—"

"Baby?"

We spun around. Miss Val stepped into view, carrying her purse and a lunch bag.

"I'm running late this morning. The twins are sick. Do you need me?"

We both went off at once.

"In the woods—"

"Derek Grayson—"

"You have to find Cameron—"

"They're trying to cover it up—"

"Whoa." Miss Val threw up her hands. "Slow down. Let's go inside and then you can tell me one at a time what happened."

She sidestepped us and unlocked her office. I didn't waste time going inside and sitting down in front of her desk. Adam stayed on his mom's heels, telling the whole story albeit in a calmer way. Miss Val froze over her chair when he said "dead."

"Dead?" she repeated. "A student has died?"

"Derek Grayson. Cam says they got into a fight, he pushed him, and Derek hit his head. He wanted me and Zeke to give him a false alibi, but we got away and came to you. We have to call the police, Mom."

"Of course we do!"

Miss Val snatched up her phone. I felt my tension finally begin to ease when she got on with the police. I couldn't bring Derek back, but at least I could make sure Cameron didn't get away with what he had done.

"We'll meet you at the front of the school. Thank you." She hung up and then turned to her son. "What's this boy's name?"

"Cameron Dupre. He's a sophomore."

She looked down at her watch. "Then he'll be in the mul- tipurpose room right now if he's trying to pretend everything is fine. The test started two minutes ago and volunteers have to help."

"The test started?" I asked.

"Yes, which means the vice principal is there now. We have to get her and tell her what's happened." Miss Val pulled Adam close and kissed his cheek. "I'm so glad you're okay, baby. Don't worry. He's not getting away with anything."

Adam spared a moment to give her a tight hug and then we took off. Miss Val marched through the halls so fast I ran to keep up, but all that mattered was that she believed us and was taking care of it.

"Stay here," she said when we reached the double doors. "I'll bring her out."

I let out a breath after the door closed behind her. "You didn't mention the others. I hope they take note of that and don't let Cameron drag them into this after all." I shook my head. "I can't believe any of this happened."

The doors opened again and I straightened.

"Valentina, what's wrong?" Argyle kept her voice low. "Is this about Ad—" She caught sight of us. "I see. Val, I'm very sorry, but I can't allow late admissions."

"This isn't about the test, but Adam was late for a reason. One of the students has been killed."

She gasped. "What? Who?!"

"Derek Grayson got into a fight and was fatally injured."

"Derek Grayson? What on earth are you talking about?"

Miss Val gestured at us. "Adam and Zeke heard the whole story from Cameron Dupre's mouth. I have the police on the way."

Argyle's eyes bugged. "Police? Val, you need to call them back right away and tell them not to come. Derek Grayson has not been killed."

I lurched forward. "I was there, Mrs. Argyle. I saw his body."

She frowned at me. "I don't know what you saw, but Mr. Grayson is alive and well. I checked him in for the test myself. He's in the room right now."

"But he can't—!"

Miss Val put a hand on my arm, containing my outburst. "Are you sure?" she asked.

"Of course I'm sure. He's sitting right there"—she pulled open the door—"front row."

Miss Val made to step inside, but I shot past her. My bursting in was ignored by most of the room except for those in the front. He raised his head and looked me directly in the eyes.

Derek Grayson.

"N-no." I staggered back, tripping over my heels, and my knees gave out. Hands caught me before I fell to the floor, but I barely noticed. The room was narrowing on a single point—a single face. Darkening around the edges as my mind fought to reconcile the limp body in the woods to this whole and perfect figure.

It couldn't be true.

"B-but he was there," I cried. "He was dead. I saw him. I saw him! He was real!"

"Wait for me," a voice whispered in my ear.

"No."

"It's me. Don't leave me."

"No!" I tossed my head so hard I smacked into his chest. "I'm not crazy! He was there!"

"Mr. Manning," Argyle hissed. "Lower your voice. The students are testing."

Adam pulled me outside. The last thing I saw before the doors closed was Derek lower his head and return to his test.

Argyle spun on us, hands on hips. "Was this some kind of prank? What would possess you to make such a horrid false claim?"

I tried to speak, but nothing would come out. I felt cold despite pinpricks of sweat covering my body. It was a deep, all-consuming chill that crept through my blood like frost spread over a window.

"This wasn't a prank," I heard Adam say. "It was a test... and we failed."

The truth of that settled in my bones. The Elite Network had tested me. They played us and Derek had been a part of it.

He tricked me.

Without a word, I pulled myself from Adam's grasp and walked away.

Chapter Eight

I didn't make it far, of course. Argyle caught up to me when I was halfway down the hall and made me and Adam go back to her office. I sat in complete silence while she told us tricked or not, we would not be allowed to take the placement test.

Derek and Cameron would be punished in the new school year with two months of detention and we would still be allowed to attend the academy. That was the best she could do and Miss Val could not sway her.

It's over. Everything I came here to do and it was destroyed before I ever really started.

"Zeke?"

Adam's voice pulled me out of my thoughts. He stood at the foot of his bed, an open duffel bag before him. It was Monday. Time to leave.

"Yeah?"

"I'm going down to breakfast. You coming?"

I shook my head. "I can wait until I go home. Besides, I don't want to see... them."

"I can't blame you." He sighed. "I'm really sorry about this."

"It's not your fault. Really, I want to thank you for being a good friend. Even though it got you into this mess."

"*You* were the good friend. A better friend than Derek Grayson deserved." He came around and grasped my shoulder.

"Despite everything, I'm glad we became friends and that I'll see you in the fall. We'll survive this place together."

For the first time in over a day, a small smile spread across my lips. "Yes, we will."

Adam left and I finally got up and pulled out my own bag. I couldn't tell him that I wouldn't be coming back, but at least we could leave things on a good note. And who knows, maybe we could still keep in touch while he was at Breakbattle and I was at Chesterfield High.

I was shoving my toiletries in my bag when a knock sounded at the door. "Adam?" I ran to pull it open. "Did you forget—"

Speech deserted me when our eyes met. For a few moments, Derek and I just stared at each other.

He took a step forward. "Can I come in?"

The question made me come alive. Anger welled up in my throat, threatening to strangle me. "No."

I grabbed the doorframe and made to slam it. Derek leaped and caught it before it closed. "Wait, Zeke! I need to talk to you."

I blinked. *What did he say? Not stalker, not perv, not cousin-lover. He actually called me by my name.*

It was that more than anything that made me pull open the door. "What is it?"

Derek pushed past me and entered the room. I turned as he found a spot on the carpet and faced me. "What happened was messed up," he said, getting to the point.

"If you believe that, why did you do it?"

He sighed. "It's been said all week, Manning. My dad is in the Elite Network and of course I knew. Every year they do a test of loyalty to make the new members prove they belong in the Network. I was ordered to go along with whatever Cameron had planned, but I didn't know until a few nights before what he wanted me to do."

"You shouldn't have gone along with it! It was sick. Twisted."

His expression remained neutral. "It was, but trust me, others have been put through worse. You have to show that no matter what happens, you'll back your brothers."

I balled my fists. "Is this why you came here? To defend your actions? Cameron's?"

"No."

"Because you can get out right now."

"That's not why I'm here. I came to say I'm sorry."

I couldn't have heard that right. "You're... what?"

"I'm sorry, Zeke." Derek closed the distance between us. "If I had a choice, I never would have done it. But I did and"—he clapped a hand on my shoulder—"you had my back. You and Moon. The Network might be pissed with you guys, but I'm hardly mad that you wouldn't have let Cameron get away with killing me. You're the kind of brother I'd want to have."

"I am?" I whispered. I didn't want it to, but somehow his words were melting the ice I forged around my soul.

"Yes. I don't care if they have a problem with it, when the new semester starts, you sit with me."

Derek released my shoulder and left. I stood there long after I heard the door click shut.

It took Adam coming back to rouse me. I kicked into gear, hurrying to pack the rest of my stuff and then scurry out of the dorms. Volunteers were waiting for us when we walked onto the front lawn reminiscent of the first day, but this time they carried envelopes.

One by one, students received their placement and then went to join their families with either whoops of glee or stony-faced silence that spoke volumes.

"Zeke Manning." She placed the envelope in my out-stretched hand. "I hope you got your desired class. Have a good rest of the summer."

I didn't open it right away. Climbing off the steps, I spotted my family and fell into Jordan's hug.

She squealed as she hugged me tight enough to make me pop. "I'm so happy to see you."

Mom bent and pressed a feather-light kiss to my forehead. "Your aunt is waiting at the restaurant. We'll eat and you'll tell us all about your week. I can't wait to add your additions to the book."

"Sounds good, Mom."

Mom turned to leave while Jordan hooked an arm through mine. We let her get ahead of us so we could talk. "So, what happened? What class are you in?"

I handed her the envelope by way of answering. I knew before she gasped what the result was. "F?! You're in the F Class? Why? How?"

"It's a long story. I promise I'll tell you everything later."

"But this is awful. What about your plan? What about"—she twisted around to make sure no one was listening—"Derek Grayson. Did you get him to trust you?"

"Yes." A smirk curled my lips, brought on by a wave of satisfaction that should have been dampened by my placement results. "He trusts me. In the end, I didn't need to get into the

Elite Class or the Network to get close to him. I'm not thrilled about being in the F Class, but none of that matters. It was always about him."

"So you're attending in the fall?"

"Oh yeah." I peered over my shoulder, letting my smirk fall upon the grand academy. "Zeke Manning will be back."

If you'd like to read the next book in the series, The Plan, click here.[1]

---

1. *http://mybook.to/ThePlanBreakbattle*

The Plan

Don't piss off the Elite Class.

That wasn't in the rulebook, but it should have been. Landon, Michael, and Cole may have the faces of angels, but a soul turns black when it's betrayed.

The Elites have sworn to take me down, but I can't get much lower.

Or so I thought.

Breakbattle wants us to fight and the boys are happy to oblige.

No one will help me. No one can. I either show I'm strong enough to rise, or I suffer at the bottom where I belong.

They'll try to break me. They may even succeed. But I can't leave. I can't reveal myself.

I became Zeke for one reason... and I'm not done yet.

Keep In Touch

Join Ruby's mailing list for news, teasers, and more:
https://www.subscribepage.com/rubyvincentpage
Join Ruby's Facebook Reader Group:
https://bit.ly/3bNuCOq

ABOUT THE AUTHOR

Ruby Vincent is a published author with many novels under her belt but now she's taking a fun foray into contemporary romance. She loves saucy heroines, bold alpha males, and weaving a tale where both get their happy ever after.